HECK'S GOLD

HECK & HOPE, BOOK 3

JOHN DEACON

Cover design by Angie on Fiverr

Edited by Karen Bennett

Want to know when my next book is released? SIGN UP HERE.

❀ Created with Vellum

PROLOGUE

H eck's Gold is book three in the *Heck & Hope* series. I recommend reading the books in order, as they tell a continuing story. If you would like a refresher, here's the story so far, along with a list of characters.

Heck's Journey (Heck & Hope #1)

Orphaned at fourteen, Hector "Heck" Martin heads west, determined to see the far country and make a man of himself.

Along the way, he falls in love with bold and beautiful Hope Mullen. But Heck is too young and poor to marry, so he heads west again.

During a three-year journey, Heck crosses thousands of miles, becomes a bareknuckle boxer, a mountain man, and an Indian fighter, and meets the likes of Kit Carson and Jim Bridger as he explores the gorgeous and deadly frontier.

Then, stopping by Fort Bent, he receives a letter that changes everything. Hope's family is daring the Oregon Trail.

Heck sets out to intercept and help them. Near the Oregon Trail in Wyoming, he throws in with another, younger orphan, Seeker, who becomes like a little brother to him.

Meanwhile, the Mullens face serious troubles—both outside and within the wagon train. When bandits attack, Mr. Mullen is badly injured, and the family loses its wagon and all their possessions. They are forced to live off the charity of the despicable Basil Paisley, a wealthy and cruel young man who wants to possess Hope.

Reunited with the Mullens, Heck saves them, kills Paisley and his thugs, and proposes to Hope, who happily accepts.

Heck's Valley (Heck & Hope #2)

As a mountain man and cavalry scout, Heck Martin handled every challenge on the Western frontier.

Now, however, he must care not only for himself but also his beloved Hope, her family, and his adopted brother, Seeker, in a remote wilderness populated by hostile Indians, bandits, and predators.

Most men would crumble under these circumstances, but Heck has enough love and courage to forge a new destiny in this mighty land. Filled with tough optimism and pioneering spirit, he vows to master the wilderness.

There is much to do.

Timber to cut. Cabins to build. Game to hunt. Land to plow and plant. A claim to stake. Caves to explore. A trading post to build. And hopefully, a happy wedding to share with the young woman he loves.

But Indians are moving through the land, and a gigantic grizzly is on the prowl. Meanwhile, 1850 brings record numbers of emigrants across the Oregon Trail. Not all are prepared, and as travel season comes to an end, a group of straggling emigrants limps into the valley, seeking sanctuary.

Heck and Hope agree to help, but not everyone should be trusted.

Most of the newcomers are good people. They bring important skills and work hard, helping mightily in the construction of the fort and the building of new roads.

Doctor Michael Skiff, who is also a pastor, marries Heck and Hope.

But newcomer Dave Chapman is secretly one of the bandits who attacked the Mullens' train and later got mostly wiped out by Heck and Seeker. He acts the part of a pleasant emigrant, but he really wants to kill Heck and steal away Hope and Amelia.

When Heck battles a giant grizzly bear, Dave shoots him in the back. Always tough, Heck barely manages to finish the bear and kill the back-shooting bandit as well.

During Heck's long recovery, he comes to rely on his friends and family, who keep things moving. Eventually, he is able to return to the mysterious cave complex, where, in the final chapter, he discovers a massive nugget of gold.

Heck's Gold (**Heck & Hope** #3) picks up the same day that *Heck's Valley* left off. Stunned by Heck's big discovery, they share the find with their family and, of course, Seeker...

Cast of Characters

Hector "Heck" Martin, 17, Kentucky-born mountain man with big frontier spirit, former bareknuckle boxing champion of the West, tall lean and powerful with a black hair and blue eyes, tough yet compassionate.

Hope Mullen, 17, Heck's wife, kind, impulsive, playful, God-fearing, great with animals, a gifted nurse with auburn hair and green eyes.

Seeker Yates, 12, Heck's adopted brother, a half-Shoshone orphan wise in the ways of the wilderness who had been wary and lonesome until he met Heck.

Mr. Mullen: Hope's father, a former boxer, tough yet quick to laugh, recently recovered from severe wounds sustained on the Oregon Trail, loves his family fiercely.

Mrs. Mullen: Hope's mother, intelligent and loving, sober-minded, follower of Jesus and often the voice of wisdom.

Tom Mullen: Hope's brother, 19, a gifted leatherworker, smitten with Amelia Haines.

Amos Johnson: a frontier bard saved by Heck and Hope after a grizzly attack, travels the West chronicling the deeds of great men.

Black Cloud: Seeker's Shoshone uncle, staying nearby, awaiting spring, when he plans to avenge the murder of his sister, Seeker's mother by Sioux raiders.

Jim Bridger: The famous mountain man, Heck's friend.

Two Bits: Jim Bridger's Shoshone employee, who "will do anything for two bits."

The Emigrants

Doctor Michael "Doc" Skiff: broad-shouldered and bespectacled, Heck's best friend among the emigrants, a man of many talents, physician, pastor, fisherman, cook.

Titus Haines: widower, former wagon master, schoolmaster, and cavalry officer.

Amelia Haines, 19, Titus's daughter and teaching assistant, likes Tom Mullen, remarkably beautiful with dark hair and brown eyes, still reeling from the death of her mother.

Susan Haines, 12, Amelia's sister.

Sam Collins: assayer, helpful.

Trace Boon: young miner determined to join the California gold rush.

Jem Pulcher: Trace Boon's cousin, equally determined to reach San Francisco.

Jacob Fox: surveyor, civil engineer, good worker.

Myles Mason: furniture maker, undertaker.

Ray McLean: Australian jack-of-all-trades, former engineer and proofreader for a women's magazine, can fix anything.

Laticia Wolfe, a.k.a. **"The Widow":** emaciated but hard a tempered steel, only hope is that her son will grow up to be a strong, capable man.

Paul Wolfe, 11, weak and timid.

Burt Bickle: freighter, hard worker, ambitious.

Abe Zale: young woodcutter with a can-do attitude.

A.J. Plum: talented blacksmith, stubborn, gets an idea and sticks to it. With him are his wife and three children, the oldest of which is nine-year-old Martin, a good little carpenter.

Gable Pillsbury: farmer.

Veronica Pillsbury: experienced midwife, Gable's wife, mother of two children.

Frank Pillsbury: farmer, Gable's brother, husband of Dot, father of four children including thirteen-year-old Franky and eleven-year-old Mary.

Mark Branch: miller.

Will Ayers: carpenter.

CHAPTER 1

"Is it real?" Mrs. Mullen asked.

Heck, Hope, the Mullens, and Seeker stood in the kitchen of the cave home with the door barred.

On the floor between them, the gigantic nugget glowed dimly.

"I think so," Heck said. "I think it's solid gold."

Mr. Mullen scratched his head and squinted as if he was having a hard time believing his eyes. "But a nugget that size, my boy."

Heck nodded. "We've hit it big."

"How much is it worth, big brother?" Seeker asked.

Heck spread his hands.

"A lot," Hope said.

"I've heard miners are getting sixteen dollars per ounce," Tom offered.

"I reckon this thing weighs a hundred pounds, maybe more," Heck said.

"Sixteen hundred ounces," Hope said, her voice soft with awe.

Heck nodded. "So, somewhere north of twenty-five thousand dollars."

For a second, no one spoke. Their eyes bulged, staring at this nugget, this inestimable fortune that had just changed everything.

"Split four ways," Heck said, "that's over six thousand dollars apiece."

"Four ways?" Tom asked.

"Sure," Heck said. "A quarter for Hope and me, a quarter for Seeker, a quarter for your folks, and a quarter for you, Tom. You spend it right, six thousand dollars in enough money to set up a nice life."

Tom just blinked at him. "But I didn't... I mean..."

"What my son is trying to say, Heck," Mr. Mullen said, "is that we have no claim on this gold."

"We want to split it with you, Daddy," Hope said.

Heck nodded then turned to Seeker. "As long as that's all right with you, little brother."

"Me?"

"Sure. They might call this place Heck's Valley, but your family was here first. Even if my name ends up on the title, this land's half yours, as is half of everything on it: grass, game, and gold."

"Partners share everything, right?" Seeker said. "And we're partners to the end. Let's split it four ways, just like you said."

Heck clapped the boy on the shoulder. "What'll you buy with your share?"

Seeker screwed up his face. "I don't know. I don't really need anything. Maybe a new hat?"

Heck laughed. "That's a good idea, little brother."

Everyone grinned with excitement—except for Mrs. Mullen, who stood there with her arms crossed, frowning slightly.

"What is it, Mother?" Hope asked.

"Sometimes, a curse disguises itself as a blessing," Mrs. Mullen said.

"A curse?" Tom said. "How could this be a curse? It's amazing."

Mrs. Mullen shook her head. "I'm sorry. I don't mean to overshadow this happy discovery. It's just—well, I can't help but notice the gleam in your eyes."

"We're excited, my dear," Mr. Mullen said, rubbing her back. "This must be one of the biggest nuggets ever found."

"I understand, dear husband. But I also know that it is *of the world*."

"So are the crops we grow," Mr. Mullen countered.

"But no one sells his soul for a fistful of carrots," Mrs. Mullen said.

"Oh, Mother," Hope laughed. "We're not putting our souls at hazard. We're just celebrating a wonderful discovery. A blessing, like you said. That's all."

"I apologize, everyone," Mrs. Mullen said. "I know you're all excited. I have no right to ruin that excitement with my speculation."

But her words had struck Heck. His gut told him she was onto something. "Hold on, ma'am. Please continue. I'd like to know your thoughts."

Mrs. Mullen looked at the others.

Mr. Mullen nodded, still rubbing her back. Her children waited, respecting their mother.

Seeker, always curious, squinted at her.

"Well, I can't help but think of Moses. We escaped disaster, just like the Jews escaped Pharaoh, and here we are, prospering in the wilderness, also like them. And by prospering, I'm not speaking of gold. I'm talking of our reunion and of this place and all that it has given us. Grass and game, shelter and fresh water. We have everything we need here, enough even to share with the emigrants."

Outside, hammers knocked in what had become the music of Heck's Valley. The thirty-one surviving emigrants were nothing if not industrious.

"But couldn't this gold just be another blessing from the Lord?" Hope asked.

"Certainly," Mrs. Mullen said. "Probably it is. And for that I am of course very thankful. But again, I think of Moses. When he went up the mountain and received the Ten Commandments, etched in stone by the very hand of God…"

"The others grew impatient," Hope said.

"And created the golden calf," Heck added.

"Yes," Mrs. Mullen said, "and worshipped the golden idol among them rather than God above them."

"Ain't nobody gonna turn this into no calf, ma'am," Seeker said.

Mrs. Mullen laughed softly and glanced at Seeker with love shining in her eyes. "I know, Seeker. But there are many ways to worship. We must guard our hearts."

"I reckon you're right, ma'am," Heck said. "I'm thankful we

found this nugget, but it might prove more trouble than it's worth. Especially if others hear about it."

Expressions shifted then, going serious as the notion sunk in. And just like that, everyone—even Seeker—understood the very real dangers posed by this incredible discovery.

If folks found out about the gold...

"We can't tell anyone," Mr. Mullen said.

"Agreed," Heck said. "I wish we could tell Sam Collins. He's an assayer, after all. He could tell us just what we have here. But we can't even risk telling him."

"Wouldn't we look silly if it turned out to be fool's gold?" Mr. Mullen laughed.

"That's right," Heck said. "But I don't reckon it will. Good news is, we don't need the money now, and it's too late in the year to cart it off anyway."

"Where would you take it?" Hope asked.

Heck shrugged. "East or west. I could find someone in St. Louis."

"Long way," Mr. Mullen said.

"Chicago's closer," Tom said.

"What about Fort Laramie?" Seeker asked. "Pa always said they had anything a man could ever want."

Heck shook his head. "Good thinking, little brother, but no one there would have this much money. It's a lot."

"Oh."

"San Francisco?" Mr. Mullen asked.

Heck nodded. "Probably best. That's where the gold is. So there should be buyers."

"But a nugget this size," Hope said, taking it all in. "That would be a dangerous trip."

"Yes, it would," Heck said, "but like I said, we don't need the money now. Maybe we never will. As is, it's like money in a bank, right? So let's just hide it away."

Everyone nodded.

"And guard our hearts," Mrs. Mullen said.

"Yes," Heck agreed, "and tell no one."

At that moment, as if summoned by his charge, a heavy knock sounded on the door.

CHAPTER 2

M r. Mullen threw a buffalo robe over the nugget, and Heck opened the door.

"Hi, Heck," Doc Skiff said, smiling broadly. "You folks have a minute?"

"Sure do," Heck said. Noting the silence, he figured he knew what was going on. He lowered his voice. "You got it?"

"We do." Doc winked.

"All right, my friend. Give us a moment, and we'll be out."

"Take your time. We're not going anywhere."

Heck closed the door and barred it, then uncovered the nugget and picked it up and lugged it deeper into the cave, where he and Hope stowed it away in the small tunnel where Seeker had hidden between his parents' death and the day Heck showed up.

As they covered the tunnel entrance with stones, Hope said, "Well, I guess we're already seeing what Mother meant."

Heck nodded. "When Doc knocked, my first thought was *hide the nugget*."

"My heart jumped like a scalded cat. And even though it was only Doc, I kept wondering if he was going to ask what we were hiding under the robe."

Heck laughed. "I guess sitting on a big old piece of gold makes a person jumpy. Nobody's gonna come demanding this or that."

"Yeah, that's clear now. But in that moment... Well, you know. It put me on edge."

"Me, too."

They started back toward the main room, where the others were waiting for them.

"What would folks do if they found out we had such a big piece of gold?" Hope asked.

"I have no idea. But some men go crazy when gold's around. They call it gold fever."

"That's a terrible notion. You don't think any of these people would try to take it, do you?"

"It doesn't seem likely, but then again, what do I know? How well do we really know them?"

"You know Doc well."

"True. I trust Doc."

"What about Titus Haines?"

"I doubt the old schoolmaster would try anything, but we've never seen the man around gold. I would be more concerned about the young bachelors."

Hope shivered. "I hope Mother's concerns come to nothing. I hope the gold ends up being a blessing, not a curse."

"Me, too, Hope, but I reckon it might end up being both."

When they went outside, all thirty-one emigrants were waiting for them. Smiles lit their expectant faces.

Looking past them, Heck saw they'd finished the sturdy-looking gate and hung it between the central guard towers.

Titus stepped forward and gave a bow. "Ladies and gentlemen, it is our great pleasure to inform you that we have completed the compound."

Heck had figured today would be the day, but it was still a pleasure to hear Titus's declaration. He had also been working hard on construction every day since his recovery and felt a little disappointed to have missed the moment of completion.

But considering what he knew was coming next, things had worked out for the best.

"That is great news," Heck said. "Wish I'd been more of a help to you. Thanks, everyone, for your hard work."

The emigrants gave a cheer.

Doc said, "You helped plenty, Heck. And besides, the only reason you didn't hammer more nails was because of the bear attack and Dave shooting you in the back. You saved us from two monsters that day."

This elicited another cheer from the crowd. Hope squeezed Heck's hand.

"If you would follow us, please," Titus said, marching toward the gates, "we will officially christen our happy home."

The grinning emigrants followed Titus, who commanded, "Open the gate."

Abe Zale the woodcutter and blacksmith A.J. Plum lifted the pine log that served as a sturdy crossbar and pushed the tall door wide.

As Titus and the others marched outside, Heck took in the place with a renewed sense of wonder.

Formed of log cabin walls and a ten-foot-tall picket fence, the perimeter enclosed a rectangular compound a hundred feet deep and nearly three times as long.

The living quarters ran along the left side and the front in a continuous, L-shaped log structure that terminated at the northern gate tower. Divided by interior walls, these quarters provided ten distinct cabin spaces.

Three of the spaces housed adult bachelors, four to a cabin. Another housed the blacksmith, A.J. Plum, his wife, and their three children. The two Pillsbury families each had a cabin. Titus Haines and his two daughters occupied another, and the Widow and her son lived in yet another.

The two remaining quarters were filled with firewood. Abe and his crew had also split and stacked expansive woodpiles outside the picket.

Additional stacks leaned against Heck and Hope's cabin and Seeker and Tom's cabin, both of which stood not far from the main vegetable garden.

To the right, they had expanded the corral to make room for extra livestock and added three large structures, including a barn for the wagons and mechanical reaper and other tools, and Badger's Trading Post itself, a long log building Heck hoped to fill with every dry good an emigrant could want along the trail.

The third building frequently rang with the sound of A.J. Plum's hammer and anvil, which Burt Bickle had rescued during his first expedition. Having the blacksmith's shop was good. With so much work going on, tools were inevitably broken. Now, A.J. Plum could fix them, and since he was also a farrier, they didn't have to worry about horseshoes.

A defensive tower stood at every corner and to either side of gate. These were crude affairs with ladders leading to elevated and barricaded platforms upon each of which four or five men could stand and fire their weapons.

It was great to see everything completed. The emigrants had taken the time to clean up all debris and tools. They'd even smoothed out the wagon paths that ran around the inside of the compound.

"Place sure has changed since you showed up, huh, Heck?" Seeker whispered, sounding impressed.

"Sure has, little brother. None of this would exist if it weren't for you and your folks."

"Shoot, I didn't have nothing to do with it, Heck. But yeah, my folks sure did. I reckon they'd like this place. I reckon they'd be impressed."

A grinning Doc stood beside the open gate. He gestured grandly with one arm, ushering them outside. "This way if you will, ladies and gentlemen."

They went outside, where the emigrants stood with expectant faces, glancing back and forth between Heck, Seeker, and something outside of the picket fence.

Heck, who knew what was coming, patted Seeker on the back and spun him around. "Have a look. What do you think, Little Brother?"

Seeker, suddenly realizing everyone was staring at him, flashed Heck an uncomfortable look. "What?"

"Look," Heck said, pointing at the huge sign he'd asked Myles Mason, the furniture maker, to create.

"What's it say?" Seeker asked.

"Come on, little brother. You've been working hard. Sound it out."

Seeker blushed but did as he was told. "F… or… t. Fort. S… Seeker. Fort Seeker? Huh?"

Heck clapped the boy on the back. "That's right, little brother. Welcome to Fort Seeker, the biggest compound between Fort Laramie and the West Coast."

Seeker's mouth dropped wide open. He just stared at the sign for a time, clearly dumbstruck. Then he swept his eyes over the high walls and the folks who'd built it and back to Heck.

"Gee, Heck, I never thought I'd have no fort named after me."

The crowd burst into wild, raucous applause.

Seeing the boy was going to cry, Heck hauled Seeker into an embrace and clutched him to his chest, saving him the embarrassment.

CHAPTER 3

"Mr. Martin," Titus said as everyone was moving back inside. "A word, please?"

"Sure, Titus. What do you want?"

As the two men paused there, Amelia, Titus's older daughter, slipped her arm into Hope's and the two of them walked off, chatting happily, followed by the younger Haines girl, twelve-year-old Susan, who had really come to life over recent weeks.

Once a shy, silent, unsmiling child, Susan had become a bubbly, animated girl who spent a lot of time staring at Seeker, who seemed completely oblivious.

"Well," the ex-schoolmaster and cavalry officer started, "I was wondering, since the fort is finished, the harvest is mostly complete, if we might speak again of school."

"Sure. What did you have in mind?"

"I know you don't approve of education, but—"

"Not true," Heck interrupted. "I just don't think education

happens solely within the walls of a schoolhouse. The business of a man's life is education. Books have their place, but these kids are learning more about frontier life by living it than they would from reading a whole library of books on the subject."

Titus gave a little nod. "Acknowledged, sir. But as you said yourself, books do serve a purpose. I'd like your permission to start holding school each weekday morning."

"I don't know about five days a week, but yeah, that might work, weather permitting."

"Weather shouldn't be a problem, Mr. Martin. Since the trading post is mostly empty at this time, I thought we might hold school inside."

"Good idea. But you missed my point. If the weather's good, these kids still need to be outside working, helping their parents and their community. The fort might be built, but plenty of work remains. Winter is coming."

"So, I may have the children when it rains or snows?"

Heck nodded. "If it rains or snows or the weather drops well below freezing, which it will for weeks at a time, you can have them for a spell on weekdays, so long as their parents agree, of course. I wouldn't expect to see Martin Plum, for example. He's learning to be a blacksmith. And I suspect many parents will need their children's help indoors, too. Cooking, cleaning, tending the little ones, that sort of thing."

"Yes, I suppose, but education—"

"You don't really want to dance around that same tree again, do you, Titus? But hey, look at that sky. Way it looks right now, I reckon you might be holding school sooner than you think. Maybe even tomorrow."

Titus studied the horizon and nodded. "It would appear so."

"All right. Good talking to you, Titus. Best of luck with the kids."

"Mr. Martin, if I might have one more word."

"What is it?"

"I was also thinking that you might consider relocating your book collection to a centralized location as a sort of lending library. We could keep them in the—"

"Not a chance," Heck said. "Somebody wants to borrow a book, all they gotta do is ask. But I'll be keeping my books in my cabin under a dry roof and a good watch."

"Yes, sir," Titus said, clearly irritated. Then he bowed and departed.

Heck was ready to track down Hope when Burt Bickle, the freighter, stopped him.

"Hiya, Heck. You got a minute?"

"Sure, Burt. What can I do for you?"

"Just had an idea is all. Been waiting till the fort was finished since folks have been using the mules and wagons to haul this and that."

"Thinking of making another trip?"

"Yessir, that's exactly what I'm thinking."

Burt's first trip had been a big success. He and a few other men had gone out with Heck's wagon and four mules and come back with an extra wagon and two big loads of important supplies the emigrants had been forced to abandon when they'd lost their stock, which had stampeded after Indians set a prairie fire for that exact purpose, nearly dooming the emigrants halfway between Laramie and here.

"If you can spare a wagon, four mules, and a few men, I'll head east again, hitch up another wagon, and bring back two more loads. Could really help us, and the folks would sure like it."

Heck nodded. "Be good for morale. What would you think of a longer trip?"

Burt chortled. "I ain't happy unless I'm hauling, Heck. What are you thinking?"

"I'm thinking maybe you and some men head to Fort Laramie instead. What would that be, an extra hundred miles each way?"

"Not even. What do you need from Fort Laramie?"

"We could use more supplies. We could ask around, maybe have Titus hold one of his town meetings."

Burt grinned. "That man loves a meeting."

"I see that. But the main thing to buy is stock. Oxen, mules, whatever you want."

A grin split his beard. "Great idea, Heck."

"With winter coming, they'll probably be happy to unload a bunch of stock. Anything beyond their own needs, I mean. Nobody else is gonna come through wanting to buy until the spring. That's a lot of feed for nothing."

"I'll bet you're right. And you know something else? They had dozens of abandoned wagons. Broke my heart, seeing all those perfectly good wagons just sitting there."

"Think they'd give them to you?"

Burt shrugged. "Wouldn't hurt to ask. I'll bet probably they would, or they'd at least sell them cheap. If I can talk a bunch of fellas into coming with me, we could bring back several wagons and supplies."

"Good thinking, Burt. Fill those wagons. I got money."

"Enough?"

"Enough. Buy as much stock as they'll sell you. But save some drivers to pick up the company's wagons on the way back. I'd like to get everyone's stuff back here, wagons and all."

"That ought to make them happy. One thing, though." Burt glanced at the darkening sky.

"Yeah, this is no country to be caught out in during a storm."

"We'll sit tight till she passes, then see how the trail looks. It'd be worth waiting for the mud to dry."

"That's your area of expertise. Do what you think is right. Muster a crew and take off when you're ready. I'll provide the wagon and the mules and some horses to ride if you get a lot of volunteers, and I'll rustle up some money and provisions."

"Appreciate that, Heck."

"And I appreciate what you're doing, running back and forth all over this dangerous country, trying to help folks."

"That's how the good Lord made me. I'm a muleskinner, that's it. You know, folks start settling these parts, even a little, a man could make a good living running freight."

"Sure could, especially if a good number of people moved in."

Burt nodded. "Man might even build a big business if he was first."

"I believe you're right. You interested?"

Burt turned from side to side, panning his gaze across the epic landscape and the jagged mountaintops clawing at the darkening skies. "It's a hard country, Heck. Hard and beautiful. Yeah, I would be interested."

"Well, then. Those wagons you bring back from Laramie, they ought to give you a start. And I'll lend you stock until you build up a stake."

"Thank you, Heck. That's mighty kind."

"You're exactly the sort of man I want as a neighbor."

"Likewise." Burt patted his shirt pocket. "But I already got a small stake. Might buy a few mules or oxen off those soldiers myself."

"Good idea."

They shook hands.

"All right, Heck. Thank you. I'm gonna go recruit enough men to do the job. Some of them might even want to buy mules of their own."

CHAPTER 4

Dark came early, wiping away the afternoon. Cold winds howled out of the north, driving heavy rain sideways against the newly christened Fort Seeker. Lightning shattered the darkness, and the heavens roared with thunder.

The storm raged on and on. From up on the ridge came the alarming sound of snapping trees. A few times throughout the restless night, boulders dislodged by heavy rain bounded loudly down the slope, cracking branches and knocking against trees.

When one of these big stones crashed down close to the palisade, the fort's namesake said, "What do you reckon, Tom? You reckon one of them boulders might come crashing down on us?"

"I don't think so," Tom said. He sat at their crude table, working a small piece of leather with the awl Heck had gotten for him from Fort Bridger. "Not this cabin, anyway. We built in a good spot."

"Well, this sure is a storm," Seeker said. "Biggest we've had since the spring. One time, just after Ma and Pa got killed, this storm come through…"

Tom listened to the boy's story, but his mind drifted back to the girl for whom he was making this little leather bag.

He loved Amelia. He hadn't worked up the courage to tell her, of course. She was so beautiful and came from an important family and had been heading toward great things in Oregon.

But yes, he loved her. Even if he didn't deserve her.

He knew Amelia was fond of him. She enjoyed their walks, talked easily, and laughed happily with him. Sometimes, she called him "her sweet Tom" or "her dearest friend."

Also, she had become good friends with Hope, which was nice.

He wished he could marry Amelia, just as Heck had married Hope here in this place.

Tom had lacked the confidence to even consider this proposition seriously, but now, holding the memory of the shining nugget in his mind, he couldn't help but dream.

Six thousand dollars was a *lot* of money. With that kind of money, he could buy land, build a house, start a real business, and provide a nice life for Amelia.

"This other time," Seeker said, laughing to himself, "a flash flood come through so fast Pa got stuck in it. This big old tree popped up and knocked him out cold, and he woke up ten miles downstream. He didn't get home till the middle of the night and had a lump this big on the side of his head." Seeker held up his fist.

"That must've hurt," Tom said, coming back to the world.

"Yeah," Seeker said. "What are you making, anyway?"

"A bag."

"For what?"

"Amelia."

Seeker grinned. "You're sweet on her."

"I am."

"You fixing to marry her?"

"I'd like to."

"She sure is pretty."

"She is. And she's a good person."

"That daddy of hers, though…"

"Yeah."

"He says I ought to go to school."

"You gonna do it?"

"I don't know. Maybe? It'd be something different, that's for sure. He's gonna hold class tomorrow over in the trading post."

"I think you should give it a shot, Seeker. What do you have to lose?"

As Tom spoke, he decided to heed his own advice. Tomorrow, he would speak to Amelia and let her know how he felt.

The excitement of Amelia blurred into excitement of the nugget and glowed at the center of his mind like a bright beacon of hope.

Faintly, he remembered his mother's warnings about Moses and guarding their hearts, but what chance could such warnings have against a young man's love for a beautiful woman?

That night, Tom lay awake a long time, listening to the rain and wind and thunder and picturing Amelia's lovely, heart-shaped face, soulful brown eyes, and glossy black hair. She had the faint ghost of a small scar on her cheek, near the corner of her mouth, and whenever her full lips spread in a bright smile, the pale pink scar lifted and bent like a dimple.

He'd do anything to taste those lips and kiss that faint scar and bury his face in the lovely midnight of those deep black locks.

He woke in the heart of the night to a distressing roar rushing outside.

He sat up straight, heart pounding. "Tornado!"

"No," Seeker's voice responded calmly from the other side of the cabin. "Flash flood."

"Will it wash us away?"

"Nope," Seeker said, "that's why Pa built up here on the bench."

At that moment, the flood rushed by outside, thundering like the voice of God.

It boomed terribly, a wave of churning water slamming down the canyon with a payload of timber and stone.

Faintly, Tom heard screams across the compound.

He rose from bed, struck a match, and lit the bedside candle. "Do you hear that screaming? Someone needs help."

Across the room, Seeker grinned. In the flickering candle-light, he looked wise and haggard, more like a weathered old man than a child. "Nah, they ain't hurt. They're just scared is all. I told you. We're safe. But you wait till tomorrow. You won't even recognize the river. A flash flood like this changes everything."

CHAPTER 5

The next morning, Heck woke before first light and sat up and slipped from bed as silently as possible, trying not to wake Hope, who stirred in the gloom and called out to him groggily. He crawled back under the buffalo blanket and kissed her back to sleep before rising again, then dressed in the darkness, grabbed his weapons, and headed out the door.

The storm had passed. Overhead, ragged clouds scudded across the sky, silver in the moonlight.

His eyes adapted rapidly to the patchy gloom, and he trudged across the compound, surveying the damage.

The buildings and picket fence still stood, though some of the roofs had probably sprung leaks.

That was all right. Leaks could be fixed. The important thing was the structures remained upright, and the high water hadn't reached the compound.

Beyond the gate, the river rushed by loudly, still swollen

after the first significant rainfall in weeks. He'd look at the river after he'd checked the rest of the compound.

The muddy ground clutched at his boots as he headed toward the corral. Branches lay everywhere, dark and twisted.

That'll be a good job for the children, he thought, *picking up all these branches.*

He stopped and stared with disbelief at the center of the corral.

Half-buried in the mud was a boulder a few times bigger than a grizzly bear. And that was just the part above the surface.

Heck lifted his eyes toward the mountain slope and imagined the enormous rock tumbling through the rain-lashed darkness and slamming down here within the compound.

It was a sobering reminder of how vulnerable they were despite their fort and rifles and all the wonderful plans streaming through their minds.

Everyone has a plan until a boulder comes hurtling out of the darkness and squashes him to a pulp.

He entered the corral and went into the stable and spoke with Red and Burly and Dolly and the other animals.

The young bull that he'd gotten at Fort Bridger trotted right out into the mud, and the cows followed, apparently unfazed by the storm, but the horses, more sensitive than their bovine cousins, remained tense in the wake of the storm. They fidgeted in the gloom, nostrils quivering, big eyes glistening like polished stones.

The mules, of course, waited for the horses to move, allowing them to bear the risk.

"Storm's over, boy," Heck said, smoothing a hand over Red's powerful shoulder, and the stallion nuzzled him, blowing softly.

Heck hooked an arm under Red's big jaw and laid his fore-head against the stallion's cheek and whispered gently into his twitching ear.

Then Heck walked out into the muddy corral.

Red followed, as Heck had known he would. The stallion's harem came next, trailed by the geldings and, finally, the mules, the last of which was Burly, who looked bored and sleepy and vaguely amused.

"You're a cagey one, old buddy," Heck said, patting Burly's shoulder. "Stretch your legs. I'm gonna go look at the river. Then I'll come back and round up some grub for you."

Heck paused at the middle of the corral and flattened a hand on the huge boulder. He could almost feel its weight.

Incredible.

Then he left the corral, crossed the compound, and headed for the gate—but stopped when he saw light spilling out from the open door of the trading post.

Now, who would that be?

In case it was an uninvited visitor, he drew his Colt and crossed the yard.

But as he drew close, he saw not a stranger but Titus Haines hard at work, mopping up the floor and readying the place for his first session of school.

Heck respected the man for getting up so early, doing the dirty work, and trying to set the place right for the kids. In fact, watching the schoolmaster swing his mop back and forth, Heck felt his heart soften.

He didn't regret disrupting Titus's early attempts at control-ling things, but maybe he'd been a touch hard on him, especially as it pertained to the school.

He tucked his pistol back through his belt and went up the stairs. "Need a hand?"

Titus turned with surprise then shook his head. "No thank you, Mr. Martin. Just a small leak, I'm happy to report. I'll have it cleaned up in no time."

"All right. Good luck today."

Titus smiled. "Thank you, sir."

Heck nodded and started to go but stopped just outside the door and turned back. "Titus?"

"Yes, sir?"

"Seeker might be rough around the edges, but don't underestimate him. Boy's sharper than an eagle's talon."

With this, Heck went back down the steps, crossed the muddy compound, and approached the gate, which stood slightly ajar.

Who had gone through?

Usually, he was the only one up at this hour except sometimes for the Widow, who confessed to sleeping poorly if at all.

He hoped it was the Widow outside. He enjoyed her company. She might be a shriveled slip of a woman, but her eyes burned like sulfur, and she was hard as granite. As he'd been warned, she kept him on his toes with her razor-sharp tongue and wit, but she never spoke without reason and always made sense.

But when he went outside, it wasn't the Widow's slender form he saw standing beside the swollen waters of the river but the broad shoulders of his best friend among the emigrants, Doc Skiff.

Doc lifted a hand. "Morning, Heck."

"Morning, Doc. How'd you sleep?"

"I've slept better. That flood came through, I thought it was a tornado."

"Not me. You grow up in the mountains, you know the sound of a flash flood. But based on all the screaming I heard, you weren't alone."

Doc chuckled then gestured toward the churning river. "This is something else."

"Yes, it is."

The water had risen to within a few feet of the bench and stretched most of the way across the canyon. Shadowy debris of great size bobbed past then swept away into the gloom.

"Think it washed out our road downstream?"

Heck nodded. "Part of it, anyway."

"Shame."

"Yeah. But we'll rebuild."

"Life on the frontier, huh?"

"I suppose. To tell you the truth, most of my time on the frontier, I never sat still long enough to build much, let alone rebuild anything."

"Well, you're doing a good job."

"Thanks."

"I mean it, Heck. You're a natural-born leader. Folks respect you. You might even say they have faith in you."

"Well, I'll try not to let them down, then."

"Are you going to stay here, Heck? Over the long haul, I mean."

"Depends. If Hope wants to move someday, I'll move. But yeah, we're sinking roots and staying a while. Maybe even forever."

"Folks have been talking."

"They do that."

Doc chuckled. "Yeah, they do. They like it here, Heck. Some of them are wondering if maybe they could stay."

"Long term."

"That's right."

Heck didn't say anything for a moment. His mind perched on the moment, feeling its significance just as his hand had sensed the staggering weight of the big boulder.

Doc let him think.

Finally, Heck said, "Would you be one of them?"

"I might be, Heck. I had my heart set on starting a practice in California. But I do love it here. It feels good, working, carving this place out of the wilderness, and I suppose I feel like I'm doing good work here."

"We're lucky to have you. And I suspect you could set up a successful practice here. If we put up a sign on the trail, you'd be hard-pressed to keep up with the demand during the emigrant season."

Doc nodded. "And the rest of the year, I'd stay busy patching up the rest of you—and fishing, of course."

Heck laughed. Beyond being a doctor and a pastor, Doc was an excellent cook and a top-notch fisherman. "Unless this flood washes away all the fish."

Doc's eyes swelled, filling his spectacles. "Don't even joke like that, Heck."

They stood in silence for a moment, watching the unbelievable volume of water flood pass.

Then, Heck said, "How many folks you think might want to stay?"

"A good number. Maybe even most of them."

Heck chewed on that for a moment, remembering what Burt Bickle had said about building a freighting business here. "They want to build a town here?"

Doc shrugged. "Maybe? I don't think they've thought that far, most of them. Though I could be wrong. They're probably picturing how they'd settle in, what they'd do. Titus probably imagines a school. The Pillsbury brothers are probably wondering how much grass is south of here. A.J. Plum is undoubtedly calculating how much work he'd get from a town and passing emigrants."

"Sounds like you folks better hold one of your town meetings."

"Will you attend?"

"Sure, if that's what you want."

"And what if they do ask to stay on?"

"It's a big decision."

"For them or you?"

"Both."

Doc nodded.

"I'll have to talk with Hope and the others."

"Of course. But I thought I'd let you know what I'd been hearing."

"I appreciate that," Heck said, and turned to head back inside. He paused and called back. "And Doc?"

"Yeah?"

"If they want to build a town here, I hope you'll stay. You're a good man."

CHAPTER 6

Heck went back to the cabin. Hope was up.

"Good morning, Mr. Martin," she said, meeting him at the door with a hug and a kiss.

"Mm. Good morning, Mrs. Martin."

As Hope fried the bacon, Heck told her about the giant boulder and the conversations he'd had with Titus and Doc.

"Well, I hope people do stay," Hope said. "Especially Amelia. You men don't mind solitude, but we females crave the company of other women."

"So you can talk about us solitary men?"

Hope laughed. "Among other things. I sure do enjoy Amelia. Do you think Titus will stay?"

"I doubt it. He had big plans west of here. I don't think he'll be happy until he has everything set up the way he likes it."

Hope nodded, looking thoughtful. "I worry about Tom. He really likes Amelia, and I know she likes him, but I don't think her father really approves."

"How can't he approve? Tom's great. What more could he want from a son-in-law?"

"I don't know. Money? Status? But where Tom's concerned, Titus keeps Amelia on a short leash. And I can see in his face that he doesn't approve of Tom."

Pacing back and forth, Heck felt a stab of irritation. "That's just stupid."

"It is, my love. Now, please sit down so we can have breakfast."

They sat and prayed and talked over food and coffee, passing the time pleasantly as so many couples have down through time. Breakfast with Hope was Heck's favorite part of every day.

She finished her food, went back to the skillet for more bacon, and sliced herself another piece of bread.

Heck smiled. "Someone woke up with an appetite."

"I really did. I've been very hungry lately. Must be all the work we've been doing. Do you think Doc will stay?"

"I'm not sure. Neither is he."

"You'd miss him if he left."

"I would. He's a good man."

"And a good friend."

Heck nodded. "Maybe I'm not quite so solitary as you think."

Hope laughed and devoured another slice of bacon.

As the sun rose outside, they discussed the emigrants, guessing who would stay and who would go.

Burt Bickle would likely stay, anchored by his dream of building the first freighting business in the territory.

Most of the bachelors, however, would probably head west

in the spring. There was, after all, a decided lack of eligible young women here.

"I hope A.J. Plum stays," Heck said.

"He's a hard worker."

"And a valuable one."

"He could do a good business during the summer months."

Heck nodded. "I don't reckon he could even keep up with the demand. If some folks stick around here, he'll stay busy enough just working for us."

"What about the Pillsburys?"

"I'm not sure. They're probably thinking about all that fertile farmland in Oregon."

"Things are perfectly fertile here."

"True, but stories have power over men's minds. They set out on the trail dreaming of paradise in the Willamette Valley. That sort of dream doesn't fade."

"I suppose you're right. I would miss the children."

"They're fun."

"They're good kids."

"They are. And good little workers."

"It would be nice if Veronica stayed, too," Hope said.

"I didn't know you and Mrs. Pillsbury were friends."

"I've barely spoken with her. But she's a midwife."

"Oh," Heck said. "Now I understand."

"Yes, that would be very nice indeed. Are you going to eat that last piece of bacon?"

"You go ahead, darling. I've had enough."

"Thanks, Heck," she said and snatched the last of the bacon from his plate.

"You really are hungry," he said. "Speaking of food, I was wondering, would you mind baking a few loaves of bread?"

"Sure. For the town meeting?"

Heck shook his head. "I want to wander over to Black Cloud's valley and see how they fared with the storm. Might as well take a gift."

"That's a nice idea. But my bread isn't as good as Mother's."

"Your bread is wonderful, Hope. Everything about you is wonderful."

Hope smiled playfully. "You keep talking like that, Mr. Martin, and—"

A knock sounded at the door.

Heck rose and opened it. "Morning, little brother."

"Hey, Heck," Seeker said. "Good morning, Hope."

"Good morning, Seeker. Can I make you breakfast?"

"No thank you, ma'am. Already had some coffee. Heck, you need me this morning?"

"Not first thing. Thought you might want to go for a little trip with me later, though."

"Sure. Where we going?"

"Thought we'd drop in on your kin. Take them some bread, see how they're doing after the storm."

Seeker grinned. "Sounds good, Heck. When do you want to leave?"

"Gotta see what folks need here first. Hope's gonna bake some bread for us to take. Probably won't leave for a few hours. You have something you want to do?"

Seeker suddenly looked sheepish. "I don't know. I was kind of thinking maybe I might see what school was like."

"Huh, I gotta say I'm surprised," Heck said. "I figured old Titus would need a shotgun to get you in there."

"Yeah," Seeker laughed, but he didn't seem amused. "It's probably a stupid idea, me going to school."

"No, it's not," Hope said, stepping forward.

"Ma'am?"

"It's not a stupid idea at all, Seeker. If you're curious, give school a try."

"Nah, Heck's right. I shouldn't—"

"Heck didn't say you shouldn't go to school," Hope said. "Right, Heck?"

Heck caught the look in Hope's eye and understood she wanted him to agree. "That's right, little brother. Go ahead and give it a shot. What do you have to lose?"

Seeker smiled with obvious excitement. "You really think I should, Heck?"

"Sure. You know how I feel about education."

Seeker nodded. "It's a man's job in life to educate himself. But you said school—"

"I talk too much sometimes," Heck said. "And that stuff I said about school, that was mostly just me keeping Titus from getting too excited. Thing is, we gotta learn wherever we are. Some folks plod through life like oxen, never learning more than they have to. But not you, little brother. You're no beast of burden. You're a young wolf."

Seeker chuckled. "Thanks?"

"I mean it as a high compliment, little brother. An oxen works all day then waits for his grain. No thinking necessary. You're not like that. You're a wolf. You live with your nose to the ground, getting by on your brains."

"And my teeth."

"That's right. But without a brain, you don't know when to use your teeth. You go ahead and try school. You might be surprised by how much you learn."

"You never went to school."

"Never had a chance."

"I went to school some," Hope said. "It was very good. I learned a lot."

Seeker looked impressed. "I didn't know you had schooling, ma'am. All right, then. Maybe I'll give it a chance. But I still want to go see my uncle and meet my kin."

"Of course. You go ahead to school, and I'll come get you when I'm ready to go."

"All right. Thanks, Heck!"

After Seeker left, Heck said, "What do you know? I think Seeker actually wants to try school."

"He does. That's why he came in asking about it. But then, when you said you were surprised, he felt self-conscious."

Heck frowned. "I noticed that. I didn't mean to discourage him."

"Seeker looks up to you, Heck. If you don't like school, a team of horses couldn't drag him there."

"I was just surprised, was all. I'm glad you were here, though. I'd hate for him to not go because he thought I didn't like the idea."

"You're a good man, Heck," Hope said, coming into his arms. "But yes, you must be careful with Seeker. Whatever you say, he takes to heart. Being a big brother is a big responsibility."

"You're not kidding," Heck said. "And you wonder why us men like solitude?"

CHAPTER 7

Later that morning, Doc stopped Heck as he was cutting across the courtyard with a sack of fresh bread thrown over one shoulder and his Hawken over the other.

"Folks want to meet tonight," Doc said. "Would that work for you?"

"Sure," Heck said. "Let's make it after supper. That way none of the cooks will have to miss the meeting."

"Good thinking. I'll spread the word. You need company on your trip?"

"I'll have Seeker with me. But if you want to come along, feel free."

"I'm curious by nature. I'd like to see an Indian settlement."

"Come with us, then. I'm fixing to grab Seeker."

"Sounds good. I'll get my rifle and be right back."

"Grab your doctor bag, too. No telling what those folks have gotten into."

"Good idea, Heck."

Heck headed for the trading post but stopped again when Burt Bickle hailed him from across the compound.

The freighter marched straight at him, churning ever forward, as was his way. "Gonna be a few days before we can head to Fort Laramie. This mud."

Heck nodded. "I figured as much. You get a crew?"

"Oh yeah. No problem there. Seven men."

"Seven?"

Burt grinned. "Yessir. Seven men, seven wagons. A man wants to build something on the frontier, he can't do it by half-measures."

"Sounds good. We'll have to get a list of things people want. We'll ask at the meeting tonight."

"Heard they're having a meeting. You know I'm in, Heck."

"Glad to hear it, neighbor."

They shook hands and parted ways, and Heck finally made it to the trading post. Walking up the steps, he heard Titus Haines's voice coming through the open door.

"That's better, Annabelle. Now, sit up straight and focus on uniformity of size. Penmanship is of upmost importance."

"Yes, Mr. Haines, sir," the voice of little Annabelle Pillsbury chimed.

Oh boy, Heck thought, *Seeker must be hating this.*

But when he reached the top of the steps and looked through the door, he was surprised to see his little brother bent studiously over his work, sitting at a makeshift table between eleven-year-old Mary Pillsbury and twelve-year-old Susan Haines.

At the far end of the table, thirteen-year-old Franky Pillsbury scratched his head and fidgeted and craned his neck, seeming to study every angle of the room that had closed around him like a cage.

He was probably admiring the craftsmanship, Heck realized. After all, Franky had done a lot of work here. He was a hard worker and good with a hammer, even though he was the oldest son of farmers, not carpenters.

Spotting Heck, Amelia stood from where she'd been helping some of the younger kids and gave a little curtsy. "Good morning, Mr. Martin."

Titus looked up sharply and gave a businesslike nod. "Children. We have a visitor."

"Heck!" one of the kids shouted, and the others chimed in, grinning and waving. "Heck! Hi, Heck! Hey, Heck, look at this scab!"

"Children!" Titus snapped, and the room went silent. "Is that how we greet a visitor? No. Everyone sit up straight and say, *Good morning, Mr. Martin.*"

The children did as they were told, although Seeker made a funny face at Heck when he said it.

"Hi, kids," Heck responded. "You be good for Mr. Haines. Come on, Seeker. Let's go see your uncle."

Heck was surprised when Seeker turned to Titus for approval.

Titus nodded. "You are dismissed, Master Yates."

"Thank you, sir," Seeker said and set to straightening his station, where he'd been working with a slate and chalk, things Burt Bickle had brought back from his expedition to the abandoned wagons.

Inwardly, Heck reeled. He'd half expected to find Titus's

scalp tacked over the makeshift blackboard and Seeker teaching the kids how to fight with knives.

Somehow, seeing Seeker act so civilized was a much bigger shock.

Oh well, Heck thought. *No harm in the kid learning about polite society, I guess.*

Seeker grabbed his Hawken from the back of the room and followed Heck outside.

"Well, little brother, how was school?"

"Good. I mean, it was okay. Not like being out in the woods hunting or something."

Heck laughed and clapped him on the back. "That goes without saying, but hey, I'm glad to hear you liked it. What did you do?"

"Well, first Mr. Haines talked to us about sitting still and being quiet, which was easy for me because I've done so much hunting," Seeker said, and launched into a detailed account of his first morning as a schoolhouse pupil.

It was mind-boggling to Heck, hearing his savage little friend so excited by what sounded to Heck like wearing a bit and harness, but he was careful not to show his surprise.

Hope was right. One wrong word, one careless facial expression, and Heck could overturn the whole apple cart. This was Seeker's business, not his, and if the boy was excited about school, so be it.

"I'm real glad you liked school," Heck said.

"Thanks, Heck."

Then they saw Doc, and the three of them set off.

Doc asked Seeker how he liked school, and Seeker surprised Heck again, responding, "It was good, sir."

Sir again? Heck thought.

Always before, Seeker had simply called their friend *Doc.*

How did one morning of schooling change Seeker so much? Heck wondered. *And why does it bother me?*

If the meeting resulted in folks staying and building a town, that would change things, too.

In most ways, it would be a help, having other folks around.

But Heck felt uneasy. After all, he had never anticipated school changing Seeker like it already had. How might the birth of a town change this wonderful valley?

CHAPTER 8

They took the long way around, following the swollen river past the old switchback trail and across the flooded pastureland until the water spread across the entire canyon and swallowed the last fifty feet of the roadway they'd built.

"Hmm," Doc said, "that is unfortunate."

"Sure is," Heck said, "but we've learned something."

"What's that, big brother?" Seeker asked.

"We've learned a road won't work here, not as things stand."

Seeker nodded. "I told you I thought it might flood."

"Well, you were right."

"What are you going to do?" Doc said. "Cut a new road up the slope farther back?"

Heck shook his head. "Too steep and twisty. We gotta stick with this one."

"But it'll just flood again," Seeker said.

"Not when we're done," Heck said. "Jacob's not just a surveyor. He's also a civil engineer. Besides, we have Ray."

"Ray can fix anything," Seeker said.

"It's true," Doc laughed. "He says solutions to tough problems come to him in dreams."

"Really?" Seeker said.

"So he says," Doc said. "Whatever the case, he gets the job done. He'll have an idea."

"Yeah, he will," Heck agreed. He had faith in the Australian's quirky ingenuity. "If he isn't too busy proofreading women's magazines, that is."

They all laughed then turned back and headed up the switchback trail. As they climbed the steep, muddy path, Heck's own mind tackled the problem. They needed to elevate the road or reroute the river. Or both.

They climbed the slope, marveling at the uprooted trees. Topping the ridge, they saw where high winds had snapped the tops off dozens of trees. Here and there, where giant boulders had rolled away, muddy craters yawned like screaming mouths.

They walked the eastern edge of the hay meadow, heading north. As usual, Heck went under the rimrock to check the iron gate that blocked the cave complex from intruders.

This time, he was in for a surprise.

"What kind of tracks are those?" Doc asked.

"Mountain lion," Seeker said. "Big one."

Heck nodded. "That's right, little brother. Judging by the size, I'd guess he's two hundred pounds or bigger."

Doc's eyes swelled. "That big?"

"At least," Heck said, then gave the startled man a grin. "Predators grow big around these parts."

"California is sounding better and better," Doc said.

"I hear the cats are even bigger out there," Heck joked.

"Hey, Heck," Seeker said, "look at this."

There, at the edge of the light falling in under the rimrock, Seeker had found the slightest disturbance in the soil, a curved line in the dirt at the edge of a stone.

"Good eye, little brother."

"That ain't natural," Seeker said.

"What is it?" Doc asked.

Heck struck a match and held it close.

"Nope, not natural at all." He backed up a step, made some calculations, and walked sideways, studying the ground, until he found what he was looking for, another partial footprint where there wasn't a stone to step on. Then, deeper in near the gate, the soil was disturbed, where someone had obviously made many tracks then done a decent job wiping them away.

"We've had a visitor," Heck said.

"Who?" Doc asked.

"Injun," Seeker said.

"Yeah," Heck said. "If they were moving this carefully, it'll be an Indian… or, more likely, Indians."

"Black Cloud?" Doc asked.

"Doubtful," Heck said, heading out of the rimrock cave and studying the wet ground outside. Tracking was difficult after a hard storm because hard weather not only obscured tracks but also destroyed patterns.

Under normal conditions, pattern recognition is a big part of tracking. Without trying too hard, a man lets his eyes rove over the ground like the nose of a hound hunting scent. Suddenly, something will break a half-recognized pattern—a mark in the ground, an overturned pebble, a few blades of grass pointing in the wrong direction—and the man's mind will zero in and read the sign with a purpose.

But a hard storm destroys the pattern. It disrupts the ground and pushes the grass every which way. Meaning you need to find something definite, a deep track.

Which Heck found after fifteen minutes of searching, fifty feet from the entrance of the cave. The hoofprint of an unshod horse.

Then he found another—and another, and another—half shod, half unshod, and called out to Seeker and Doc.

The Indians had ridden out of the north and paused here before carrying on to the south.

At least he thought they were Indians. If all the tracks had been unshod, he would have known they were Indians, but the shod tracks made him wonder.

Were some of them riding stolen horses? Or was this a mixed group, perhaps scouts and Indians riding together?

Whatever the case, there had been a few riders. Probably four or five.

Who were they? Where had they gone? What did they want?

"We can visit Black Cloud tomorrow," Heck said. "We'd better get home and let folks know about these tracks."

CHAPTER 9

That night, Heck and Hope, Seeker, and Amos Johnson joined the Mullens for supper in the main cave.

Heck and his family agreed the emigrants were good people who would, if they chose to stay, improve things in the valley—but a town would add problems as well.

Amos sat at the end of the table, jotting notes in his secret shorthand as the family sorted out their thoughts on the matter. He hadn't offered any opinions.

"What do you think, Amos?" Mr. Mullen asked.

Amos shrugged. "I'm just glad I'm here to record all this. If this becomes a big town someday, folks will want to know how it all started."

When supper was over, Hope said, "I can hear people gathering out there already."

"Let's sit here a bit longer," Heck said. "Let them talk among themselves first."

No one objected, though Tom looked a little twitchy, no doubt excited to see Amelia.

So Mrs. Mullen made a pot of coffee, and they waited a while, talking among themselves. When they finally went outside, the courtyard was full.

The emigrants turned expectantly toward them.

Heck and Doc exchanged nods, but of course it was Titus who stepped forward to speak for everyone. Titus stopped ten feet from them and stood very straight and swept his gaze back and forth as if he were standing on an elevated stage. "Mr. and Mrs. Martin, Mr. and Mrs. Mullen, Mr. Johnson, Thomas, Seeker, thank you for joining our town meeting. Several among our number hereby petition—"

"We know what you want," Heck said, cutting him off. He might have committed to giving the guy a break with his school, but nobody born and raised in the mountains could stomach circuitous pomp. "A bunch of you want to stay, right?"

He addressed the question not to Titus but to the whole group. As he swept his gaze over them, many heads nodded.

"But a lot of us are still heading west next spring," Trace Boon, one of the young miners announced.

"Yeah," Jem Pulcher, Trace Boon's constant companion said. "No offense, folks. We sure do appreciate everything all'y'all've done for us."

"No offense taken," Heck said. "I expect most of you will be moving on. Whatever drove you westward, it's still out there, waiting for you. And besides, there aren't exactly a lot of eligible young ladies to choose from here in the valley."

This earned laughter and more nodding.

"Not yet," Abe Zale spoke up. The woodcutter was one of

the young bachelors but apparently had his own view on the situation. "We don't know who will move into this valley over the next year or two. I mean, you folks probably never guessed you'd have thirty-some guests for winter, did you?"

More laughter, more nodding.

"You got that right," Heck said. "But we've enjoyed having you folks here. That first day, Doc promised me you'd work, and you've sure done that."

Heck spread his arms wide, indicating the whole of Fort Seeker. "We sure have accomplished a lot since you arrived. And we could accomplish a lot more if some of you stay. So, who among you is still planning on heading west in the spring?"

In addition to the two young miners, six others raised their hands—and the hand of Titus Haines meant that two whose hands did not rise, Amelia and Sarah, would also be leaving, taking the total to ten.

Heck glanced at Tom, who looked like he'd been punched in the stomach.

Beyond the miners, the schoolteacher, and his family, they would lose five bachelors: Will Ayers, the carpenter; Mark Branch, the miller; Myles Mason, the furniture maker and undertaker; Sam Collins, the assayer; and the Australian jack-of-all-trades, Ray McLean.

What a staggering loss of talent.

Heck nodded. "All right. Who wants to stay?"

Three hands rose. Then, after a sharp glance from his mother, young Paul Wolfe timidly lifted his hand, too.

Heck smiled and looked back and forth, making eye contact with each of the four people and saying each of their names. "Widow, Paul, Burt, Abe, consider yourselves officially invited to make your homes here with us in this valley. We'll be happy to have all of you."

Burt Bickle clapped his hands together and laughed. "Thanks, Heck. Bickle Freighting will be famous all over the West!"

"That's what I'm thinking," Abe said. "We have a real opportunity here. Next year, tens of thousands of people will pass by. There's a lot of money to be made. It won't be in firewood. I know that. There isn't enough timber here. But the way things are, I could get rich even if I set up a shoeshine stand."

"I don't care about money," the Widow confessed. "I like you folks. I trust you. And I know this place will make a man of Paul. That's all I care about. We left nothing in the East and were heading toward an equal portion in the West. This place is our home now."

"We'll be real happy to have you, ma'am," Heck said. Then, glancing at those who hadn't declared their plans, he said, "I guess the rest of you haven't made up your minds yet?"

He saw nods all around. Among the undecided were Doc, A.J. Plum and his family, the Pillsbury clan, and the surveyor, Jacob Fox—seventeen people in all.

"Well," Heck said, "we'd be happy to have any or all of you, but if you decide to move on, we'll do what we can to help you get where you're going."

"Bickle Freighting will deliver both goods and persons for a reasonable fee," Burt joked, getting a few laughs.

"Thanks, Heck," Doc said, speaking up at last. "You folks saved our lives. There are no two ways about that. And I know I speak for everyone when I say we'll be forever grateful."

They all set to nodding.

"Personally, I'm conflicted," Doc said. "I still dream of California, the fish I might catch in the Pacific, and yes, unmarried women I might meet there. But I do believe you will build a wonderful little town here... and not just because of God's bounty and the amazing resources of this valley but also because of the people you are. You set a very high standard for those who would settle here."

More nodding.

"You have plenty of time to make up your minds," Heck said. "In the meantime, Jacob, would you help us mark out lots for the Widow, Burt, and Abe?"

"Sure, Heck," the surveyor said. He was a likeable young man who never seemed to tire.

"How much are you asking for land?" Gable Pillsbury asked.

"I'm not," Heck said. "I'm going to mark out lots, and folks can live there for free as long as they like."

"But they can't sell that land," Hope qualified.

The farmer's eyes lit up. "If we stayed, could we work some bottom land?"

Heck nodded. "Of course. I'm also thinking of moving cattle into the valley. I'd need help managing them."

"We could do that," Gable's brother, Frank, said.

"Well, you folks figure out what you want to do and let me know," Heck said.

"Could we get what you said in writing?" Jem Pulcher asked, the notion of free ground apparently causing him to rethink his decision to head west. "How you'll lease it to us and all, I mean. Could we get that in a contract?"

Heck leveled his gaze on the young miner. "You got something better than a contract, Jem. You got my word. But let me be clear. I'm offering this land now, not indefinitely. We strike a deal, that's it. You stay as long as you want, rent free, and reap what you will."

Excitement rippled through the assembly. Folks exchanged glances full of meaning.

"But you holdouts," Heck said, "I reserve the right to change my mind anytime. Like Abe said, next spring, folks are gonna pour into this land. And when they see what we have here, well, I expect some will offer good money to buy into this valley. They'll have a lot to offer, skill-wise, too. So if you decide you want to stick around, see me sooner rather than later. If we're gonna build a town here, we're gonna do it right."

CHAPTER 10

When Titus Haines's hand had risen, the air rushed from Tom's lungs. Then, watching Amelia's hand rise, Tom felt like his heart might stop.

They couldn't leave…

For the rest of the meeting, Tom barely heard Heck and the others. He could only stare at Amelia and reel at the thought of losing her.

Amelia offered a sad smile then wiped at her eyes.

When the meeting broke up, Tom walked over and asked if he might have a word with Amelia.

Mr. Haines stared at Tom the way he always did, with a look that blended contempt and suspicion.

"Would that be all right, Father?" Amelia asked.

Mr. Haines frowned. "Don't be long, Amelia. You must help Susan with her Latin."

"Yes, Father."

Titus turned, dragging his younger daughter with him. Susan cast an admiring smile at Tom over her shoulder.

Tom waved at the little girl, then turned to her lovely sister.

"Amelia," he said, then the words he'd been meaning to say stuck in his throat.

"Oh, Tom," Amelia said, "please walk with me."

Tom nodded, and they walked away from the others, craving privacy. He led her to the steps of the trading post, where they could talk.

To Tom, Amelia looked lovelier and more precious than ever. He felt desperate, felt like he might explode.

"I'm so sorry, Tom. I didn't know Father had made up his mind. I would have told you if I'd known."

"I don't want you to leave, Amelia."

Amelia's soulful brown eyes filled with tears. "Oh, Tom, I hate to leave. Not this place so much, but you. I can't bear the thought of losing you."

Sudden emotion strangled Tom. He reached out and seized her hand in his.

She looked surprised at his boldness but did not pull her hand free. "What if Father sees?"

"Then I'll tell him the truth."

She blinked up at him, her long lashes sparkling with tears. "The truth?"

"I love you, Amelia."

Her pretty mouth opened slightly, and Tom heard the sharp intake of breath.

"It's true, Amelia. I love you. I have loved you from the first time I set eyes on you."

"Oh, Tom, I—"

"Please let me finish, Amelia. I didn't say anything because I didn't want to startle you. I thought we had time. Now your father says he's leaving. Well, I'm sorry if I did startle you, Amelia, but it's true. I love you."

Amelia blinked up at him, saying nothing, her expression troubled.

As her silence stretched out, an icy hand formed in Tom's chest. If she denied him now, if she said she didn't love him, that claw would tear his heart to shreds.

Amelia bit her lip, and fresh tears filled her eyes.

Tom squeezed her tiny hand. "Amelia, please say something."

"Oh, Tom. What can I say? I love you, too. You must know I love you, Tom."

Her words filled him instantly with joy, and suddenly, just like that, anything seemed possible.

Then she said, "But Father made up his mind. You heard him. We're leaving."

"I have to be with you, Amelia."

"I won't leave Father and Susan. They need me. Since Mother died—"

"I would never ask you to leave your family," Tom said, "but what if I left mine?"

CHAPTER 11

After the meeting, Heck and Hope retreated to their cabin.

"I thought that went well, Mr. Martin."

"Likewise, Mrs. Martin."

"How many do you think will end up staying?"

"Hard to say. I figure winter will dissuade a bunch. Then, when spring comes and the grass starts popping up, the West will start calling to them again."

Hope nodded thoughtfully. "I wish Amelia was staying."

"I wish she was, too, Hope. I know you've gotten to be good friends."

"We have. But I wish she was staying for her and Tom, too. She didn't look very happy when Titus raised his hand."

"No, she didn't."

"I feel so bad for Tom. For Amelia, too. I had hoped they would make a permanent match."

"They should elope," Heck joked. "Doc's cabin is only two doors down."

"I don't think Titus would approve."

"No, I doubt he would. But spring's a long way off. Who knows? After teaching for a while, maybe he'll settle in."

"I sure hope so, Heck, because otherwise, poor Tom is going to be heartbroken."

"I'm glad your folks never gave me a hard time."

"They both loved you instantly. It didn't hurt that the first time you met Mother, you carried us to dry ground and saved our carriage. And then with dad, of course... well, he loved you from the start, as if you were his own son. You should have seen how excited he would get whenever we received a letter from you. He cheered every victory as if he were standing at ringside."

"I sure am thankful for your folks," Heck said. "I felt the same way about them right from the start. The way they took me in and gave me a fresh start, without that kindness, I never would have made it. And if your pa hadn't gotten me started boxing, I'd still be in St. Louis, scrounging for pennies."

"No you wouldn't," Hope said. "That's not your nature. You're too strong and smart to stay down for long. You would've found a way."

"Well, I appreciate your confidence, ma'am, but St. Louis is a hard town. Seems to me cities are good at keeping poor folks poor. Most of the people I knew back there were worn out from working all the time but still didn't have two pennies to rub together. Plus, you pack people together, throw up a bunch of buildings, folks can't even see the horizon anymore. It's easier to dream big out here in this country. You climb up to the top of the ridge and look off west toward the mountains, watch the snow blow off the jagged peaks and glitter in the sun, well, you feel like there's nothing in the world you couldn't do if you put your mind to it."

Hope smiled at him. "I love it when you talk this way, Heck. It's like poetry."

Heck snorted at that. "Well, I'm no poet, my love. That's for sure. And just to prove it, I gotta go take care of Dolly and the boys."

"Well, thank you for tending to my horse, Mr. Martin. Would you care for some coffee when you get back?"

"Yes please, ma'am."

He kissed her then went out into the courtyard and headed for the corral to take care of Dolly, Red, and Burly. Other folks now cared for the rest of the animals, but Heck would always care for his own.

"Heck, do you have a moment?"

Heck turned to see the Pillsbury brothers, Gable and Frank, standing there.

"What can I do for you men?"

Gable, the older of the pair, stepped forward. "We was talking, Heck, and we reckon we might want to stay."

Frank nodded.

"I'm glad to hear that," Heck said. "A town will need farmers. And when babies start coming, it'll be good to have Veronica here."

Gable nodded. "Sooner or later, folks always need a midwife."

"You mentioned lots," Frank said.

"And bottom land," Gable quickly added.

"That's right," Heck said.

"How much land you reckon you'd let us have if we stay?" Frank asked.

"We'll work it out. Maybe forty acres apiece?"

"And you won't charge us rent?" Gable asked.

Heck shook his head. "You work the land, then sell or trade the crops and keep the profit. Of course, if folks are hurting…"

"We wouldn't let nobody starve," Gable said.

"Only forty acres, though?" Frank said.

Heck looked at him. "That's not enough?"

Frank licked his lips. "We was hoping for maybe a couple hundred acres apiece."

Heck grinned. "A couple hundred, huh? So, four hundred acres for the two of you. Of bottomland, no less. For free."

"We was just thinking, was all," Gable said.

"Right," Frank said. "We didn't mean no harm."

"Well, if my offer isn't good enough for you, feel free to head West in the spring. I'm sure you'll find a better deal out there somewhere."

CHAPTER 12

The next morning, Amelia woke early and opened her eyes and smiled into the darkness, savoring her memory of the previous evening.

Tom loved her. He really loved her. So much that he was willing to leave his family and head to Oregon with hers.

It was all so romantic.

She rose and got around and went outside. It was a chilly morning but dry and pleasant in its way. The brisk air brought her fully awake, and before heading back inside, she paused there for a moment, enjoying the solitude and the soft, almost tentative sound of birds out there in the gloom, greeting another day.

Tom loved her!

She remembered how surprised she had been when he'd seized her hand, and then how she'd surprised even herself when, parting for the night, she had kissed his cheek.

If father had seen that…

She shivered a little but smiled.

Father hadn't seen it. And now, when she told him that Tom would be accompanying them, Father would see that Tom was a man of conviction.

Would she and Tom be married?

The mere thought stole her breath. The notion was staggering, yet it pleased her.

She did love her sweet Tom. And he was respectful toward Father and kind to Susan. A real gentleman, Tom was.

And talented, too, she thought, clutching the little leather purse he'd made her.

She felt a rush of joy and reentered the cabin. Moving as quietly as she could, she added a stubby log to the fire and set to making breakfast.

When the bacon began to sizzle, Father woke.

Susan slept on, of course. Having overcome the terrible loss of Mother, Amelia's little sister was a bright flame of a girl again. It warmed Amelia's heart. But the girl slept deeply and woke reluctantly.

When breakfast was ready, Father took a seat on the crude chair he'd made by placing a cushion atop a short log and faced their even cruder table, a sheet of canvas tacked to several similar logs all pushed together. The table was just large enough to accommodate the three of them if no one pushed his or her plate fully onto its surface.

"Well, I suppose you should wake your sister," Father said.

"Actually, Father, would it be all right if we let her sleep just a while longer? I had hoped to have a word with you... privately."

Though Amelia suspected her mention of privacy had awakened Susan, who was probably lying there with her eyes shut, listening hard. The girl loved nothing more than eavesdropping.

Oh well. It didn't matter to Amelia. She wished she could share her news with the whole world.

"All right," Father said and sipped his coffee. "What's on your mind, darling?"

Happiness filled her like warm sunlight. "I just wanted to share the most wonderful news, Father."

Father raised a dubious eyebrow. "Wonderful news about what?"

"About Tom. He—"

"Wonderful news about the Mullen boy? What could possibly be wonderful about him?"

"Oh, everything, Father. But what I'm trying to tell you is that Tom wants a future with me."

"A future? With you? That's preposterous. Forget it, Amelia. As soon as the spring grasses arise, we will continue west as planned."

"Tom says he'll come with us," she blurted. "That's how much I mean to him."

"What sort of man would leave his family to chase a woman so far above his station? Is he delusional?"

"No, Father. He cares for me. He—"

"In Oregon, you will find plenty of young bachelors, men of education and independent means."

"I have no interest in them, Father. I care only for Tom. He's so kind—and he's incredibly talented with leather work."

"Then he'll make a fine employee someday. Better to marry

the man who sells the leather, my dear, than the one who works it. Don't you want a good life?"

"Yes, Father, and Tom—"

"Tom is convenient. He's here. Nothing more. The only reason I've allowed you to spend time with him is to help you overcome the grief of your mother's passing. But I know you, Amelia, know you even better than you know yourself. You have expensive tastes, darling. You like fine things—and you shall have them in Oregon. Given your upbringing and education and beauty, you could be a great woman in the West. You will marry well, marry into money, and join the leading society of a new land. Doesn't that notion excite you?"

She shook her head, fighting the tears that stung her eyes now. "Father, I love him. I love Tom."

"Love him? Oh, Amelia. He's just a boy. He'll never amount to anything. How could he? He comes from peasant stock and lives here, penniless, on the charity of Heck Martin."

"Much as we do, Father."

Father's eyes flashed, and his face went bright crimson.

"I'm sorry, Father. I didn't mean to—"

"Enough. Thank you for bringing this matter to my attention. I never would have expected you to behave so recklessly, but now that I understand, we will nip this little problem in the bud."

"Father, no. Don't forbid me to see Tom. You can't. Please."

He sighed, leaned back, and crossed his arms over his chest. "Fine. If we were back East, I would forbid you to see him ever again. I'm surprised at you, Amelia, engaging in such foolishness."

She wanted to stand up to him, wanted to tell him that it

wasn't foolishness, that she loved Tom and he loved her, but she held her tongue, because she knew if she persisted in saying those things, he might forbid her from seeing Tom after all.

"Here, however," Father continued, "that would be rather difficult. It might even cause serious trouble with Tom's family. That father of his might act friendly, but his nose and knuckles tell me he's a rough-and-tumble sort. Not that I fear such a man, you understand. I simply don't want trouble, especially since Mr. Mullen and Heck Martin are clearly good friends. And no surprise there. Heck's hands carry even more scars than Mullen's. Therefore, you may remain friends with Tom."

Amelia bowed her head. "Thank you, Father. Thank you very much."

"But you are forbidden to entertain any ridiculous notions of love. This relationship will never go beyond chaste friendship. Do you understand?"

"Yes, Father."

"And if I sense you are entertaining anything beyond friendship, I will forbid you from seeing him, even if doing so results in my having to thrash that fighting rooster father of his. I will not have my daughter marrying a commoner with no prospects for advancement."

CHAPTER 13

Heck climbed the switchback trail slowly, scanning the ground for any sign of the Indians who'd passed through the valley recently.

But neither he, Seeker, nor Doc spotted anything as they scaled the steep slope. Reaching the top of the ridge, they fanned out, cutting for sign as they crossed the field. They found only the tracks they'd seen before.

And that was good. Heck hoped he never saw any sign of those Indians again.

From the hay meadow, they headed northwest through the woods.

Heck and Seeker moved silently over the carpet of bright yellow leaves, but Doc scuffed along, apparently oblivious to how much noise he was making.

"Sir," Seeker finally said, "if you pick up your feet and put 'em down every time, they won't scuff so loud."

Doc's mouth dropped open. "My apologies. I didn't realize what I was doing."

"No problem, sir. And I'm sorry to go telling you your business. It's just that in country such as this, walking loud can get a man scalped or shot or eaten."

"Or all three if you run into the wrong tribe," Heck said and slapped Doc on the arm.

Doc nodded soberly, and from that point forward, they moved much more silently through the forest, which was easier than it would have been before the storm. The still-damp eaves didn't rustle or crunch like dried-out leaves would have.

Descending into Black Cloud's valley, Heck paused halfway down the slope, scanned the forest, and listened hard, flaring his nostrils and scenting the breeze.

Nothing. Not even smoke from a campfire.

That was strange. He would have expected Black Cloud and his people to keep a fire going here, since it was a cold morning, and there were no nearby threats.

Unless, of course, Black Cloud had seen the Indians who'd ridden across the hay meadow. If that was the case, he would have extinguished his fire and hidden his family.

At the base of the slope, a narrow, swift-running stream made it difficult to hear anything else.

Heck pointed to the muddy marks high up the bank where a flash flood had torn through this valley. It had to have been fifteen feet high.

This was more of a ravine than a valley, with even steeper slopes than in Heck's Valley. The speed and force of the flash flood must have been shocking.

"Look," Doc said in a grave voice and held up a muddy little ball.

"What is it?" Heck asked.

"A child's moccasin," Doc replied soberly.

The implications punched Heck in the gut.

"Do you think they're okay, Heck?" Seeker asked.

"I sure hope so. Their camp must be upstream. A flood like that might've surprised them."

The three of them stood there for a moment, staring at the muddy little shoe like it was a bad omen. Which Heck feared it might well be.

But then a voice said in Shoshone, "You found the missing shoe. My wife will be pleased."

They turned, and there stood Black Cloud, thirty feet away just uphill from them, cradling in his arms the rifle Heck had given him.

"Everyone's okay?" Heck said.

Black Cloud nodded. "And your people?"

"We're okay. The flood washed out our road, though."

"That is good. Roads bring more people. No offense."

Heck grinned. "None taken."

"If I am not mistaken, you have brought me more bread."

"It's true. My wife baked it."

"In return, I will provide information. Just before the storm, four riders crossed the ridge behind your home."

Heck nodded. "Two horses shod, two unshod."

Black Cloud frowned. "Now I have nothing to trade."

"That's all right, my friend. The bread is still yours."

Black Cloud smiled. "You are a good neighbor. Come, say

hello to my family. They will be happy to see you, especially Seeker. We are half a mile upstream."

As they walked with him, Heck said, "Half a mile? How did you know we were here?"

Black Cloud turned to Doc and said, "Do you speak Shoshone?"

Doc smiled uncomfortably and asked Heck what Black Cloud had said.

"He's inviting us to visit his family. He's happy about the bread."

"Oh," Doc said, gave a little wave and continued to scuff through the leaves alongside them.

"I have chosen this one's Shoshone name. He will be known as *Walks Like Buffalo*."

CHAPTER 14

The next day was Sunday. Everyone gathered in the courtyard, and Doc led the service. The congregation stood while singing the hymns, then sat upon hides, blankets, chairs, stools, and logs.

Susan Haines sat beside Amelia on a deer hide. It wasn't very comfortable because of a rock poking up from underneath, but she tried not to move, because fidgeting would anger Father.

He had been cross ever since talking to Amelia the previous morning. Amelia had stopped crying, but she was still very sad.

Susan felt bad for her sister. Tom was nice and funny and good-looking. No wonder Amelia was sad.

But Father was right about Amelia. She did like nice things.

Was he also right about Tom, then? Would Tom be able to afford those nice things that Amelia liked so well?

Susan didn't know. But she liked Tom and wished he had a little brother. Then he could be her boyfriend.

When Amelia had been twelve, boys liked her. But no boy ever paid attention to Susan.

It wasn't fair.

But that wasn't Amelia's fault.

Susan reached up and rubbed her sister's back.

Amelia offered her a sad but grateful smile and leaned in and hugged her and then kept an arm draped over her shoulders as Doc read from the book of Ezekiel and talked about idolatry and abominations and God's wrath.

Unlike her sister, Susan was glad they were moving on in the spring. She was thankful for everyone here. Heck and the others had saved them, she knew, but that didn't mean she wanted to live here forever.

She would never have a boyfriend here.

Glancing to her left, she saw the Pillsburys clustered together.

Franky could be her boyfriend. But he insisted on treating Susan like a little girl.

It was infuriating.

So Susan was excited for spring and Oregon. She wanted to live in a house again and wanted friends and a nearby town where she could go and see things and Father might buy her a piece of candy or a new dress.

More than anything, she wanted Mother back, but she wouldn't allow herself to dwell on that desire, because thinking about Mother always made her cry, and she had to be strong now, for Amelia.

It was very unusual for Susan to be in this position, the stronger sister, the comforter, and she was determined to do a good job and help Amelia through this hard time.

Her twelve-year-old heart latched onto this duty and soared at the notion of helping her eighteen-year-old sister in a time of need.

But then they were standing and singing again, and church was over, and Amelia excused herself and Father had to talk to the men about rebuilding the road, so Susan was alone.

The children called her over, telling her to join them for games.

She was about to accept when she saw Franky walking away.

Impulsively, she called to him.

"Huh?" Franky said. He turned and saw her. "Hi, Susan. What do you want?"

"The kids want to play some games. Since you don't have to work today, I thought maybe—"

He grinned and waved her off. "I'm going fishing." With that, he turned and started to walk away.

She called to him again.

He turned. "What?"

"Why do you always treat me like a little girl?" she demanded.

Franky Pillsbury shrugged his big shoulders. "Because that's what you are."

"I am not. I'm only a year younger than you."

"Really? Huh. You seem a lot younger. I thought you was maybe ten or eleven." The way he said it, she could see he wasn't teasing. He meant it. He really had thought she was that young. That stung.

"Well, that's just stupid," she said.

"Hey, look, Susan, I don't want to play. You go have fun, all right? But I'm no kid anymore. I'm going fishing."

"I could go with you."

"Yeah, right," Frank laughed, as if she'd been joking. "That's a good one, Susan. Have fun with the other kids."

And just like that, he turned his back on her and walked away.

Susan stomped her foot. That Frank Pillsbury! She was no kid. Someday, he'd realize that. Someday, she'd be tall and pretty like Amelia, and her figure would fill out, and then Franky would wish he'd been nicer!

"Hey, Susan," Franky's eleven-year-old sister said, catching Susan's arm. "Come on. Let's go play!"

"Thanks but no thanks, Mary," Susan snapped, jerking her arm free. "What do I look like to you, a kid?"

Mary's eyes swelled with surprise. "What's wrong, Susan? I thought you said—"

"Well, you thought wrong. I'm not a kid anymore, Mary. Go have fun with the little ones. I'm going to go read a book."

"Okay, Susan," Mary said sheepishly. "Have fun."

Susan marched off, feeling bad. Mary Pillsbury was nice. Unlike her brother.

That Franky!

Susan felt bad that she'd been so cross with Mary. Half-turning, she glanced back over her shoulder, hoping Mary wouldn't still be standing there, crying or something. If so, Susan would feel terribly guilty.

But Mary had already run off and joined the other children, who were racing off together without so much as a quizzical look in Susan's direction.

So maybe Franky was right. Not about her being a little kid. But about there being a difference. Maybe that's why the little kids didn't call to her now, trying to get her to change her mind and join them. Maybe they sensed it, too. Maybe there really was a difference. Maybe she had passed out of childhood into young womanhood.

Yes, that was it. She was no longer a child. She was a young lady. So now she had to start acting like it.

Maybe if she quit playing with the kids and started acting differently around Franky, he'd see her for who she really was, who she was becoming, who she would be.

Maybe then, Franky would fall in love with her the way Tom loved Amelia.

Her face grew hot at the thought. It was confusing and exciting, and she would never confess to anyone that she had even entertained the thought.

But now she was stuck. If Franky wouldn't take her fishing, and she wasn't supposed to play with the kids, what could she do?

She had lied about reading, of course. She did have a book, a collection of fairy tales by Hans Christian Andersen, but she didn't feel like reading and especially not some kids' book.

So then... what would she do?

She stood there at the center of the courtyard, feeling suddenly alone and exposed and curiously vulnerable, like a field mouse about to get snatched up by a screeching hawk.

But she was no mouse. She was a young lady. And she must decide what to do.

Spying the trading post, she had an idea. It appealed to her but also ashamed her because it was somewhat childish.

But at least no one would see her.

And besides, in a way, she was merely preparing for her future. And that was a very mature thing for a young lady to do with her free time.

She entered the trading post and closed the door and for the next several minutes marched back and forth, pretending this was her classroom and that the room was full of boys and girls, her students.

"Please pay attention, Franky," she admonished the invisible boy. "How do expect to learn if you don't—"

Susan gasped, hearing voices outside. Grownup voices! What if it was Father? What if Father caught her playing in here?

She quickly scrambled under Father's desk, which was actually a table with a sheet of canvas serving as a tablecloth.

The door opened. She heard footsteps as people entered. The door closed again.

Leaning close to the floor, Susan peered out from beneath the canvas and saw the shoes of two people standing close to each other near the door.

It was Amelia and Tom!

"Tom, sweet Tom, I don't know how to tell you this," Amelia said, and by her voice, Susan could tell she was crying. "It's... Father..."

"What is it, Amelia? He didn't hurt you, did he?"

"No, nothing like that. Not physically. Oh, but he did wound my soul."

Susan listened, barely breathing, knowing what was coming next. Her heart fluttered in her chest, pumping dread and glee in equal measures.

Not that she would ever wish such misery on her sister. It was just exciting to be here, listening, at such a moment.

"What is it?" Tom asked. "I wondered why you avoided me yesterday. The night before, when we parted, you seemed so happy."

"I was, Tom. I was so happy, happier than I've been in my whole life. But everything's changed."

"Why?"

"Father says I'm not allowed to court you."

"What? You can't be serious, Amelia."

"I am serious, sweet Tom," Amelia wept.

"But why? What did I do? Is it because I grabbed your hand?"

Susan felt a thrill. Tom had grabbed Amelia's hand?

"No, he has no idea about that, Tom. Father has always been... set in his ways, I guess. He has a certain view of the world. And certain expectations for me."

"What expectations?"

"He wants me to marry a rich man, someone who can provide a nice life for me."

"Oh," Tom said and fell silent.

He was quiet for a long time. Was he hurt? Angry?

Oh, how Susan wished she could see his face, but she couldn't push herself forward that much, couldn't risk getting caught. Amelia would kill her!

"Tom," Amelia said, "say something, please."

"So, if I had money, your father would allow me to court you?"

"It's terrible, Tom. I know it's terrible, and I'm so sorry. He's just—"

"Amelia, I'm going to tell you something, but you have to promise not to tell anyone."

Susan's heart leapt with fresh excitement. Tom was about to share some big secret!

"You can tell me anything, Tom," Amelia said. "And you know you can trust me. I won't tell anyone."

"Well," Tom said. "There's something no one knows. You see…"

CHAPTER 15

Heck stood with Ray McLean and Jacob Fox alongside the downstream from Fort Seeker.

Where their road had run only recently, now the bank was washed away, leaving a muddy depression and debris.

"It's quite a mess," Jacob said.

"You got that right," Heck agreed. "Question is, what do we do about it?"

"The Army Corps of Engineers would dig this out, put in heavy pilings, and build an elevated ramp to connect the two sections of roadway," the young engineer said.

Heck nodded. "I thought of something like that, but we don't have the resources."

"I'm sorry, Heck. I know the old path is steep and full of twists and turns, but I think it's still our best bet," Jacob said.

"I don't know," Ray said, speaking for the first time since he'd agreed to come out with Heck and Jacob. The Australian tilted his head, eyeing the devastation with a thoughtful expression. "I reckon we could build a levee. It would need to start back a ways, well behind where it washed out this time, back before the river cuts in."

Heck glanced upstream at the bend, picturing it. "You want to redirect the river?"

"Something like that," Ray said. "It shouldn't be too hard. We're certainly not lacking for stone, and we've got all those big timbers we hauled out of the river after the flood. Heavy stuff. Pile it up real good, backfill it with dirt and more stones, sturdy stuff. Then use it as the main path for the livestock, pack it down real good. We do that, I reckon it ought to withstand a flood. You might end up with some repair work each spring, but it beats starting all over again."

"Sure does," Heck said and felt a thrill, recognizing one of those magical moments when Ray cooked up a surprising solution to a difficult problem.

"Besides," Ray said, "it's not like we have to reroute the whole river. We just need to coax this stretch a bit to the east."

Ray led them back upstream to the bend. He stood there for a moment, studying the river, then turned to look back downstream, and Heck knew the man was seeing the job as if it were already finished.

"Yeah, that would work," Ray said. "We'll need a lot of stones right here," he said drawing an imaginary line coming off the bend. "Then we'll fill it in with timbers and dirt. We'll have to get the angle right."

Jacob nodded. Heck could see the engineer conceptualizing Ray's plan and getting excited. "If we come out at too sharp of an angle, the next flood will demolish the levee."

"Right," Ray said. "The levee will have to stretch out a bit.

We'll have to figure out exactly how far. Not too long. Shouldn't be a problem at all, really. The river will have all summer to change its course through here, and we can keep plugging away, building up the space between."

Ray led them back to the muddy mess downstream. "Then, back this way, we can build a ramp, get the road up good and high."

"Lot of work," Jacob said.

Ray shrugged. "Less work than it'd be rebuilding this road every time there's a flood."

"Agreed," Heck said. "But are you sure we could do it, Ray?"

Ray fell silent for a moment, twisting back and forth, surveying the whole scene, then shrugged. "I reckon we can sort it out."

"I'm happy to hear that," Heck said. "Have you ever built anything like this before, Ray?"

The Australian grinned like a madman. "Where would be the fun in that, mate?"

CHAPTER 16

From that point forward, the men of Heck's Valley worked hard on the levee from dawn till dusk.

Three days in, however, two of the men took a break.

"You're kidding," Trace Boon whispered, leaning on his shovel.

Jem Pulcher spat into the mud. "I never kid about gold."

They stood a little way off from the other men, who were hard at work rebuilding the washed-out road.

Trace considered his companion for a second. He'd known Jem a long time, his whole life, practically. They had grown up together in Pennsylvania and were cousins, though everyone thought they were brothers because they were always together and looked alike.

So Trace knew Jem was telling the truth.

Gold was the one thing neither one of them joked about. It had possessed their minds ever since they'd first heard of the big strike in California. From that point forward, they worked like mules, trying to build up enough money to head west. And this spring, when they'd finally saved enough, Trace and Jem had borrowed a wagon from their uncle and headed west, bursting with gold fever.

Then, tragedy struck. First, cholera hit the wagon train. Then, Indians set a fire and drove off their stock.

Now, they were stuck here in Heck's Valley until next spring. And they both lay awake at night worrying the gold would run out before they made it to California.

But now, Trace thought, the heat of excitement spreading through his chest. *Now...*

"A hundred pounds?" he asked, finding it impossible to believe.

If Heck, who was no miner as far as Trace knew, had already found a hundred pounds of gold, there must be a fortune in this valley. A hundred fortunes. A thousand.

Jem nodded. "That's what they say."

Something inside Trace jumped with excitement.

A second later, however, doubt crept in.

A hundred pounds of gold? It was too much, too wonderful to even imagine. And besides, Jem hadn't seen the gold himself —and Trace knew Jem could get a little excited sometimes. "Who told you?"

Jem looked from side to side. "Mark. He heard Franky telling his dad. Said the kid was all excited."

"How'd the kid know?"

Jem shrugged. "No idea. But Mark said the kid was sincere."

"Well, maybe Franky was sincere, but that don't mean he was right. Some other kid probably pulled a prank on him."

"Maybe, but I don't think so, Trace. I got a feeling."

"Well," Trace said, going back to shoveling. "You take another look at that feeling, I think you'll realize you're suffering from a case of gold fever."

Jem shook his head and spat again. "Nope. It's here, Trace. This is it. This is why everything happened. All the bad stuff. The Asiatic cholera. The prairie fire. All of it. So we could end up here."

Trace smiled with more confidence than he felt. "So… what, you think destiny brought us here?"

"Destiny, fate, God… I don't know. But that's why we ended up in this place. For the gold. It's here, Trace. I can feel it in my bones."

"Well," Trace said, forcing a laugh that didn't sound genuine to even his own ears. "Your gut, your bones. Your body sure is chiming in this morning. All of it except your brain, that is. Tell me, if this place is made of gold, where is it? I mean look at all this mud. Where's the gold, Jem?"

Jem made a face. "You know how gold works. You find some here, some there. But not everywhere. Besides, there's mud on everything. Look at that rock. Just looks like a clump of stone. There could be gold all through here, it wouldn't glitter."

Trace realized he was nodding. Jem was making sense. "It does explain something."

"What's that?"

"Heck."

"What do you mean?"

"You ever meet somebody so confident?"

"Not by half. But then again, he's pretty rugged."

"Rugged, sure, but it's more than that. The way he acts, it's like he's above worry."

Now, it was Jem's turn to nod. "You're right. He does seem that way, like he isn't even capable of worrying."

"Which makes sense. If you had a hundred pounds of gold, what would you worry about?"

"Somebody taking it."

"That's about the only thing." A smile spread across his face. "Sure would be nice."

"You mean it *will be* nice. I'm telling you, Trace. This is it. This is our destiny."

"But how do we get in on the gold?"

"We go over right now, tell Heck we changed our minds, we want to claim some land here, make this our home."

"What if he puts us up on the ridge? Only gold up there is the hay."

Jem smiled. "Thought about that. We're gonna tell him we changed our minds. Not just about staying. We decided we want to be farmers, like the Pillsburys."

Trace nodded. "Heard he offered them forty acres apiece."

"Yeah, bottom land with river frontage. Which means they can pan."

"I like the way you think, cousin. Let's go get on this before the word spreads and other folks get the same idea."

They threw down their shovels and shook on it and headed toward where Heck was piling rocks between the river and the road.

CHAPTER 17

"Something's going on," Heck told Hope that night after supper, when they were finally alone in their cabin again.

"What do you mean, Heck?"

"The gold. I think folks know."

Hope's eyes swelled. "What happened?"

"Few things. First of all, the Pillsbury brothers both decided to stay here and asked if they could claim the forty-acre lots I'd offered."

"Well, that makes sense, doesn't it? I mean, they came to their senses."

"That's what I thought at the time. But then, fifteen minutes later, Trace Boon and Jem Pulcher came over and said they'd also changed their minds. They wanted lots, too. Said they'd decided to become farmers and wanted to know if they could have lots with river frontage."

"Maybe they heard about the Pillsburys and thought things through. I mean, free land is appealing."

He nodded. "But then they asked what if they found something on the property. *Something like what?* I asked them, and they acted real jumpy and said, *Oh, you know, something good, something like silver or gold.*"

"Seems like a question miners would ask."

"Right. But the Pillsburys asked the same thing."

"They did?"

"They did. And you should've seen how eager they were, waiting for me to answer."

"What did you tell them?"

"I said they could work the land, and any crops they raised were theirs, but any gold was mine."

"And how did they react?"

"Gable and Frank looked disappointed. Jem and Trace, they looked crushed. I asked them did they still want the land, they said they'd think about it."

"So they really just wanted to hunt gold."

"Sure seems that way. I noticed people looking at me differently today, too. Like they had never seen me before. Reminded me of how, back when I was boxing in St. Louis, folks would look at me when they heard I was an undefeated fighter. Their eyes would light up with interest. Kind of a mix of admiration and fear but mostly just curiosity. Sometimes, especially among big men, there was a question in their eyes, like they were wondering if maybe they could take me."

"This is terrible," Hope said. "You really think people know?"

Heck nodded. "Unfortunately, yes."

"But who would have told them? You know I wouldn't breathe a word."

"I know that, Hope, just as you know I wouldn't."

"Mother wouldn't. Daddy wouldn't."

Heck nodded. "And Seeker wouldn't share our secret, not even under torture."

Hope looked mortified. "But that means... you don't think... not Tom."

Heck spread his hands.

"Tom would never share our secret," she said, but her eyes went out of focus for a moment. "You don't think he'd tell Amelia, do you?"

"That's what I'm wondering. I mean, her daddy said he's leaving, right? What if Tom tried to talk her into staying. He's crazy about her."

Hope nodded. "He is. He loves her. But still... do you really think he'd do such a thing?"

"If he was only telling Amelia? Maybe. I mean, it's not like you and me have many secrets."

"That's true. But even if he did, who would Amelia tell?"

"I don't know."

"Not Jem and Trace or the Pillsburys."

"No, but she might tell her daddy if she thought it would endear him to Tom."

Hope just stared at him for a few seconds without saying anything then frowned. "Do you want me to ask Tom if he said something?"

"No, ma'am. If anybody does the asking, it'll be me. But I don't see myself doing that. This could still be coincidence—though I doubt it—or maybe there's something we're not thinking of."

"Like maybe someone found a nugget in the river?"

"Exactly. But I do think folks know there's gold. Now, I'm just wondering how that's gonna change things around here."

Hope crossed her arms over her chest, looking worried. "Oh, Heck, everything was going so well."

"It was. And hopefully, it still will. But I reckon we'd best take this bull by the horns before he hooks us."

"What do you mean?"

"I have a plan."

"To find out who told?"

"No. To find out what those who know about the gold are fixing to do about it."

CHAPTER 18

The next day, as Heck led the work crew back out to the big construction project, Hope and the women she'd rallied went upstream to pick more apples and forage wild burdock roots. Hope had made the outing sound like a party, and the women were all smiles when they left, accompanied by Doc and Mr. Mullen, who agreed to stand watch.

Only Titus, Amelia, and their pupils remained behind in the school. Otherwise, Fort Seeker was empty.

Heck threw himself into the work, figuring his test would come to nothing. But people were still acting strangely, and after fifteen minutes, when Jem Pulcher hobbled over, clutching his stomach, Heck quit unloading rocks and pretended to believe the miner, who said he had a horrible gut ache.

Jem was a pretty decent worker, most of the time, and might know a thing or two about mining, but he was a terrible actor.

"I'm sorry to hear that, Jem," Heck said. "Why don't you head back and rest for a while. Want me to help you get home?"

"It's all right, Heck. I'll help him," Trace said and slipped an arm around his cousin's back. "Come on, buddy. I'll take care of you."

"All right," Heck said. "Good luck, you boys."

They struggled toward home. Jem remembered to stay bent over for fifty feet or so. After that, Trace dropped his arm from his cousin's back, and the pair walked swiftly toward the fort.

Heck waited for them to disappear around the bend, then told the other men that he had to go check something.

"Want me to come along, big brother?" Seeker asked.

"No thanks, little brother," Heck said, picking up his Hawken. "I got everything I need. I'll be right back."

Unlike the miners, he'd ridden to the worksite, so he mounted Red and headed for the fort, taking his time, not wanting to surprise the pair before they had time to get inside and incriminate themselves.

He rode through the gate, climbed down from Red, and ground hitched the stallion. Seeing no sign of the men, he glanced toward the bachelors' cabin.

The door stood wide open, which was normal on a mild day like this one with plenty of sun and a light breeze. If men were going to share a small cabin, airing it out from time to time was a great idea.

But neither Jem nor Trace were inside their cabin.

That's because they were in his.

Heck heard them through the door, which stood slightly ajar. He heard thumping inside. The men spoke rapidly in hissing tones.

He leaned his Hawken silently against the wall, drew his Colt, and pushed through the door.

Jem and Trace were rooting through his things.

Trace gave a terrified yelp and bolted for the door. Which was stupid, since Heck was standing just inside it. But fear makes fools of men, and Trace was determined to shoot from that door like a rabbit trailed by hounds.

Heck lashed out with his left and smashed a powerful jab into Trace's jaw.

Trace ran straight into it. His head jerked back, and his legs went out from under him, and he spilled to the hackberry planking.

"Wait," Jem said. "Don't hit me. I can explain."

"You don't need to explain," Heck said. "I know exactly what's going on here. You boys heard I had gold, so you figured you'd sneak in here and steal it."

"No," Jem blurted. "We weren't gonna steal it. We would never rob you, Heck. You gotta believe me. We just wanted to see it, was all."

"You just wanted to see it?"

"That's right," Trace said groggily and staggered to his feet, rubbing his jaw. "We came west to hunt for gold, but we never saw none before, other than necklaces and rings and coins and such. None that come out of the ground, I mean. So we figured we'd come back and take a look."

Heck looked back and forth between the men. Surprisingly, he believed them. Not that he would let them know that. They'd stepped way over the line, and he wasn't going to let them off the hook that easily.

"I caught you rooting through my home. I'm well within my rights to shoot you both between the eyes."

"Don't do it," Trace said. "I'm telling the truth."

"Yeah, don't shoot us, Heck. We never would have took it."

"One at a time, Jem first, use your left hand to pull that pistol out of your belt. That's it. Nice and easy. And don't get any bright ideas. Time like this, bright ideas get men killed."

"Yes, sir," Jem said and drew the pistol slowly from his belt.

"Set it on the bed. No, the other end. That's it. And don't start wondering if you can spin around with that thing and beat me, because you can't. That's it. Now step on back. Trace, it's your turn."

After the men had disarmed themselves, Heck gestured toward the door with the muzzle of his Colt. "Outside. Don't try to run. I'll be right behind you with my finger on the trigger and every reason in the world to pull it."

Once they were all outside, Heck pushed them toward the trading post.

"Can't we just forget this, Heck?" Jem said. "We told you we didn't mean nothing. We was curious, that's all."

"How did you know about the gold?" he asked them.

"Mark Branch," Trace said without the slightest hesitation.

"And who told him?"

"Mark overheard Franky telling his dad," Jem said.

It definitely seemed to Heck like they were telling the truth. And their story would explain why the Pillsburys had come to him first and asked about finding gold.

But again, he wasn't through with them. Not by a long shot.

"How did Franky know?" he asked them.

"No idea," Jem said. "That is the truth, Heck. We got no idea. We just heard, was all."

They reached the schoolhouse and Heck told them to sit on the ground and warned them again not to run or try anything stupid. Then he walked up the steps and knocked on the door.

Amelia opened the door with a bright smile. "Hello, Heck."

Behind her, the children chimed, "Good morning, sir."

Franky was not among the children, of course. Like Seeker, he was out doing a man's work.

"Morning," Heck said and gave them a wave with the hand that wasn't clutching a revolver. "Titus, a word, please?"

"Yes, Mr. Martin," Titus said. "Amelia, please attend to the class while I speak with Mr. Martin."

"Yes, Father."

Heck followed him outside and quickly explained that he'd found the men rooting through his cabin.

"We wasn't gonna take it, Mr. Haines," Jem said.

"Honest, we wasn't," Trace said. "We just wanted to see it, was all."

"See what?" Titus asked, visibly annoyed, then turned to Heck. "What on Earth are these nincompoops babbling about?"

"You haven't heard the rumors?"

Titus scowled. "What rumors?"

"Heck's got gold," Jem said. "That's what they say."

"Yeah, a hundred pounds," Trace said.

Hearing those words, Heck felt a sinking sensation. Any doubt that one of his family members had shared his secret now vanished. Until this moment, it could have been coincidence. Franky could have lied, or someone could have told him a lie, or maybe someone had found a spot of color and assumed Heck had found some, too... but Trace and Jem knew it was a hundred pounds of gold.

Titus scowled. "I'm far too busy teaching children to swap such ridiculous rumors."

"It ain't that ridiculous," Heck said. "I do have a hundred pounds of gold."

Titus's mouth dropped wide open.

"But nobody was supposed to know about it," Heck said. "Now, help me tie them up."

Titus, having recovered from news of the gold, returned to his officious self, lifting his nose and staring down at Trace and Jem with obvious contempt. "Certainly, sir."

"Tie us up? What for?" Jem asked.

"Come on, Heck," Trace begged. "We was just curious, was all. We didn't hurt nobody."

Heck regarded them grimly. His quick mind had been firing all this time, and he had come to an important conclusion.

This was a milestone moment in the formation of the town he might build here. This pair had committed a crime. How he handled it would echo down through however many years folks lived here.

If these men had raped or killed, Heck would put a bullet through their brains and be done with it.

But they hadn't done anything like that. He suspected they were telling the truth about just wanting to see the nugget, but they had still entered his home without permission.

How would this town punish such behavior?

He wasn't sure, but he knew that answer would carry consequences of its own. All across the West, fledgling communities' responses to lawless acts were determining the character of those communities and the expectations of their citizens.

"You boys broke the law," Heck said.

Jem's face twisted with irritation. "Law? What law?"

"The Law of Heck's Valley."

"What's that mean?" Trace asked.

"That's what we're fixing to find out."

CHAPTER 19

Once everybody had returned to the compound, Heck explained what had happened.

Trace and Jem started to protest, wanting to tell their side of the story, but Heck told them to pipe down or he'd gag them.

"You'll get a chance to talk, but we're gonna do this right."

The men fell silent. Jem looked angry. Trace looked terrified.

"I believe in law and order," Heck told everyone. "Not just philosophically but pragmatically. A lawless society never prospers. It begets only chaos, which leads to feudalism."

Several people looked deeply confused.

"If there aren't laws," Heck said, rephrasing it for them, "might makes right. The strongest do whatever they please, and the weak can't do anything about it."

Now, everyone nodded.

"Law can't be capricious," Heck said. "It has to be consistent.

It has to protect the lives and rights and property of law-abiding citizens. Any corruption of that would be an abomination."

No one disagreed.

"If we're going to build a town here," Heck said, getting to the point, "we're gonna have to have laws. We have to figure out how we handle incidents like this."

"Hang 'em," A.J. Plum volunteered. "All thieves should be hung."

A few folks nodded. Others shouted against the blacksmith's suggestion. Most folks just looked frightened.

"Hold on, everybody," Heck said. "We gotta do this right."

"Whatever we decide," Doc spoke up, "it will become part of us, part of any town we build here."

Heck nodded. "We gotta decide how we want to live. Not just today but moving forward. We need to have that talk now, before we sentence these men and deliver them unto justice."

All around the courtyard, people nodded. Jem and Trace looked understandably terrified.

Tom looked pale and sick.

"Amelia, my dear," Titus said, "perhaps you should take the children back inside."

"Yes, Father."

"I ain't going nowhere," Seeker declared. "This here is my home. I want a say."

Heck nodded in agreement. "And Franky, I'd ask you to stay, too."

"Yes, sir." The large boy, he noticed, looked every bit as pale and sick as Tom.

As Amelia marched the small ones off to the trading post,

Frank Pillsbury spoke up. "So is it true, Heck? You really did find gold?"

Across the courtyard, folks' faces did many things. Some were clearly surprised or confused. Others regarded Heck with twinkling eyes and eager expressions.

"Yeah, I found gold," Heck said.

Murmurs filled the courtyard.

"A hundred pounds?" Pillsbury asked, his eyes glittering.

"Don't really know what we have," Heck said then turned to Sam Collins, the assayer. "Later, Sam, maybe you can help me figure that out."

"Sure thing, Heck."

"Here's the thing, Frank," Heck said, returning his attention to the farmer, "what we found doesn't matter. Trace and Jem busted into my cabin without my permission. And that's what we need to talk about now."

"No civilized society allows burglary," Titus suggested. "In fact, any society that allows burglary to go unpunished can no longer be referred to as civilized."

"I happen to agree," Heck said. "What about you folks?"

All agreed.

"But we wasn't gonna take nothing," Trace whined. "That's the truth."

"How come you went into the man's cabin, then?" A.J. Plum demanded. "I catch anybody rooting around my shop, I'll crack his head open with a hammer."

"Seems to me," Ray McLean offered, "these blokes might be telling the truth. Maybe they heard something and got a stupid idea in their heads. Curiosity killed the cat and all that."

"But they did enter his home without permission," the

Widow said. "That alone seems like a criminal act to me. If I'm ever so lucky as to build a home here, I don't want people just going in and looking through my things whenever they feel like it. So regardless of whether they intended to actually steal anything, we need to decide the consequence for such actions."

"String them up," A.J. Plum said. "Make an example of them. We won't have any more trouble with thieves."

"Don't do it," Tom said, stepping forward with a desperate look on his face. "People make mistakes. I'm sure they're sorry. Show them mercy."

Heck gazed at his brother-in-law, who had almost certainly started this whole mess. "Some people can't handle secrets. They hear something, they make a mistake. Then people get hurt. Maybe even killed."

"I do think my son has a point," Mr. Mullen said. "These boys had no right to enter your cabin, Heck, but if we kill them, we'll have committed the bigger sin."

Hope nodded, agreeing with her father. "We can't kill them for sneaking into our cabin."

Heck nodded. "I happen to agree with both of you. But what if they'd snuck in there and murdered us in our sleep?"

Hope gasped.

"We never would've done something like that!" Trace shouted.

"I believe you," Heck said, "but the question stands." He panned his gaze across the many faces staring at him. "What will we do to murderers?"

"Kill them," A.J. Plum said, and several voices called out in agreement.

"I can live with that," Heck said. "Cold-blooded murderers should be executed. Anyone disagree?"

No one spoke up, though a few looked downright sick.

"What about rape?" Heck asked.

"Death," the Widow said.

Her voice hung in the air with steely finality.

"All agreed?" Heck asked.

All did.

"What if two men voluntarily engage in a conflict, and one is killed?" Doc asked.

"Justifiable," Burt Bickle said. "Two men want to fight, let them fight. That's the law of the West."

A few people disagreed, but the overwhelming majority agreed with Burt.

"Most of us find that justified," Heck announced. "So that's the way we'll handle it in this valley."

"What about accidental homicide?" Abe Zale asked. "We were out in the woods once back in Ohio, and one fellow swung his axe at the wrong time and killed his friend."

"If anything like that ever happens," Doc suggested, "I think we'll have to handle it on a case-by-case situation."

"Agreed," Heck said. "Everyone?"

Everyone nodded.

"What about theft?" Jacob Fox asked.

"Thieves should be put to death," A.J. Plum said. "It's one of the ten commandments. Thou shalt not steal."

"As is *Thou shalt not covet*, Mr. Plum. Would you execute the covetous? Have you never wanted something that wasn't yours?"

"That's different," Plum said.

"Which proves my point," Mrs. Mullen said. "God's commandments should be honored, but not necessarily enforced by death. If I'm not mistaken, Mr. Plum, I heard your hammer and anvil on the sabbath."

A.J. Plum turned red at that. "Yes, ma'am."

"What's stolen matters," Doc suggested. "Stealing a horse is a lot worse than stealing a slice of bread."

"So you're suggesting we have a scale?" Heck asked.

Doc shrugged. "Or a range of consequences, anyway."

"It's a complicated question," Heck said. "How many agree thieves should be punished?"

Everyone but Trace and Jem raised their hands.

"And how many agree that stealing a horse is worse than stealing a slice of bread?"

Everyone agreed again, though A.J. Plum said, "But a thief is a thief. You let him get away with stealing a slice of bread, he'll be stealing horses in no time."

"He's got a point," Gable Pillsbury said.

Several people nodded.

"So we'll need real consequences no matter what is stolen," Heck said.

"Maybe this is better left until later," Hope suggested. "The scope of the scale, I mean."

"I think you're right," Heck said. "We can all talk among ourselves and sleep on it and reconvene in the coming evenings. Figuring this stuff out is gonna take some time, and that's all right. We want to do it right. When you get down to it, we're talking about the heart and soul of our community.

Whatever laws we agree to, they won't just govern us, they will define us."

All around the courtyard, folks nodded solemnly.

"So what do we do with these men?" Titus asked, redirecting everyone's attention to Trace and Jem.

CHAPTER 20

"How do you men plead to the charge of breaking into my cabin?" Heck asked. "Guilty or not guilty?"

"We already said we did it," Jem said.

"Guilty, then," Heck said.

"To going in," Trace said quickly, "but not trying to steal anything."

"Right," Jem said.

"As it so happens," Heck said, "I believe you. Hope, do you believe them?"

Hope regarded the two men thoughtfully. "I guess so. But they never should have gone into our cabin."

"Agreed," Heck said. "But we'll drop the charges of theft. As to invading our home, they have admitted their guilt, so there is no need for a jury. All that's left is the consequence."

"Banishment," the Widow said.

"Agreed," A.J. Plum said. "If you won't hang them, put them

out. And keep their guns so we don't have to worry about them exacting revenge."

"You can't put us out this late in the year with no guns or horses," Jem said.

"Yeah," Trace said. "We'd die."

"Should've thought of that before you broke into their cabin," Plum said.

"I do think they would die out there," Heck said. "How many want to banish them anyway?"

Folks raised their hands.

"Opposed?"

Other folks raised theirs.

It was much closer than Heck had expected. That closeness surprised him and underscored the importance of what they were doing here.

"When we first came here," Doc said, "you told us how it was going to be, Heck. And I remember at the time thinking it was eminently logical. Your valley, your rules. What do *you* think we should do with them?"

Heck looked at the two men awaiting his judgment. He held his stare for a moment, wanting them, wanting *everyone*, to understand and remember. "I don't think we should banish them. I've killed a lot of people. Dozens of them. Many were close enough that I could watch the life fade from their eyes."

People squirmed and murmured.

"I have no qualms about killing men," Heck said, "or sentencing them to death by banishment."

Trace started crying. Jem looked murderous.

"But I will not kill indiscriminately. Death must be justified. And in my opinion, these men did nothing deserving death, whether that death comes by way of hanging or banishment. They need to apologize to Hope, set the cabin right, and serve double guard duty for a month."

Trace sighed with relief. Jem grinned.

A.J. Plum and others grumbled.

"And," Heck continued, "I'm gonna punch them both in the stomach."

Jem quit grinning. Trace looked worried but nodded.

Around the courtyard, some folks looked horrified.

Heck understood. It was, after all, a brutally visceral punishment, like a penalty out of the stone age.

But despite A.J. Plum's severity, the blacksmith was staring an unfortunate reality in the face. In a perfect society, men would govern themselves. Trouble was, someone always messed that up. A certain type of individual—more of whom would come West with each passing year—would only follow the rules out of fear of punishment.

Heck didn't want to kill these men. But he didn't want them or anyone else to forget that real punishment awaited those who did not respect the sanctity of others' homes and property.

A punch to the gut was more fitting than a bullet to the forehead or a slap on the wrist.

Jem seemed more inconvenienced than concerned. Which made sense. He was young and strong and had probably taken more than a few punches in his time.

But not from Heck.

"Go ahead," Jem said crossly and walked over with his hands still tied behind his back. "Let's get this over with."

Heck nodded, twisted back, then swung his right fist in a powerful uppercut that pounded into the surly man's stomach.

The punch lifted him off his feet and dropped him to the ground, where he curled up, mouth gaping and closing, unable to breath, eyes as round and distraught as those of fresh-caught cutthroat trout lying on a stony shore.

After several seconds, Jem finally gasped, breathing again, but it was a long time before he had the strength to get to his feet.

Those who'd scoffed about Heck letting these men off with a light sentence stood in awed silence now.

Next, a terrified Trace stepped up. "We didn't mean nothing by it, Heck. Really. It was just gold fever. It made us crazy, made us stupid. We—"

Whatever he'd been going to say was knocked out of him along with his breath, and then he was down on the ground, too, his body too shocked to even draw breath for several seconds.

Most people looked shaken. It was one thing to talk of death and banishment. But to stand there and see men punched, to hear the sounds, and see them stretched on the ground, unable to breathe... well, that sort of abrupt, efficient violence tended to make an impression.

Which is exactly what Heck intended. Because only with that sort of impression lurking could mercy and goodwill reign. People had to know there was an edge.

Franky Pillsbury turned sharply away and vomited.

"All right, folks. That's it. Justice has been served."

People broke apart and started drifting slowly in their separate ways.

Doc lingered for a second, giving Heck a wary look. "You're a different sort of fellow, Heck."

Heck shrugged. "I just try to do what's right."

"I know. That's it, I guess. I don't know many folks who could weigh issues of crime and punishment intelligently, argue for mercy, then deliver such savage blows with their own hands."

"Did I do right, or did I do wrong?"

"Oh, you did right," Doc said. "I'm just glad it wasn't up to me."

"We're all in this together, Doc. We'll get it done."

Doc nodded, still eyeing him almost warily. "With you leading us, we just might do that, Heck. We just might after all."

They parted, and Heck called out to Sam Collins, who was sort of hanging around not far off, probably waiting for Heck to say something. "Hey, Sam. Have a minute?"

"Sure thing, Heck. Want me to take a look at the gold?"

"That's right. If you'll wait here, I'll go get it ready. I'm not gonna bring it out and stir folks up. But I'll call you in when it's ready, okay?"

"Sounds good, Heck. I'll be waiting."

Heck joined Hope, who was waiting for him halfway to the house where her parents lived—and in the caves of which they had hidden the nugget.

"You handled that well, husband," she said, slipping an arm through his.

"Thanks, Hope. I take no pleasure in it, but I reckon it had to be done."

"You're right. If we're going to build something here, we have to establish law and order we can all live with."

"Man, you really knocked them for a loop," Seeker said, joining them. He threw back his head and laughed with the characteristic lack of decorum Heck loved. Somehow, it cut straight through the tension. "Man, that Jem, he thought he'd gotten off easy until you nailed him. His feet hopped about six inches in the air!"

As Seeker launched into another laughing fit, a soft voice called from behind, "Heck, could I have a word, please?"

Heck turned, and there stood Tom. There was no color in his face, and he looked on the verge of tears.

CHAPTER 21

"All right, Tom. What do you want to say?"

Tom glanced at Hope and Seeker then back at Heck, desperation in his eyes. "Could we talk privately, Heck, just you and me?"

"All right, Tom. Let's go into my cabin." He gave Hope's arm a little squeeze and released it. "I'll meet you inside the cave shortly, Hope."

"All right," she said, and her voice sounded faint, almost afraid. "Heck?"

"Yeah?"

"Please…"

"Yeah?"

She just stared at him for a moment. He saw many things in her emerald eyes. She loved her brother and was worried that Heck was going to hurt him.

But she said nothing, perhaps because of the other thing

Heck saw in her eyes: trust. No matter what came, Hope had faith in her husband.

"I love you," she finally managed.

"I love you, too," he said, and turned to deal with her brother.

Heck opened the door and held it for Tom, who walked in before him. Then Heck followed him in and shut the door behind him, and gloom descended upon them, the cabin lit as it was by a single window.

"Heck," Tom said. "I have a confession."

"I know you do, Tom."

"You do?"

"Yeah, I do. But you go ahead and say the words."

"This was all my fault."

"What do you mean?"

"What happened today with Jem and Trace. I caused the whole mess."

"Did you tell them?"

"No, of course not, Heck. I would never do something like that."

"But you told somebody."

Tom nodded and dropped his eyes to the floor. "Amelia. Heck, I'm sorry. I shouldn't have said anything. I know that I—"

"Why, Tom? Why did you tell her? We were all sworn to secrecy."

"I know, Heck, and I'm so sorry I betrayed your trust. If I could do it all over again, I wouldn't say a word, I swear."

"Trouble is, we can't do things over. Plenty of men out here will kill for gold, you know that, right? What if they'd come in here at night and killed your sister and me?"

Tom lifted his face and stared at Heck with a horrified expression. "That's what I kept asking myself out there. That and what if you decided to kill them. When A.J. Plum suggested hanging them, I panicked."

"So tell me, Tom. Why did you do it? Why did you tell Amelia?"

Tom shook his head. "When Mr. Haines said they were leaving, I told her I'd go with her. She told her father, and he told her we could only be friends. He said in Oregon, he planned on her marrying a wealthy man."

"So you told her you had some money coming."

Tom's pale face nodded. "I'm sorry, Heck. I love her. I couldn't bear the notion of just being friends. I know it was wrong to tell her, but you have to believe me, she's the only person I told."

Heck nodded. "I forgive you, Tom. I wish you hadn't done it, but all is forgiven."

Tom exhaled a big breath and smiled weakly. "Thank you, Heck." He shook his head. "I never thought Amelia would have told anyone."

"I don't think she did. You saw how surprised Titus looked when he heard about the gold. Who else would she have told? She didn't mention it to Hope, and they're best friends."

"But if she didn't tell anyone…"

"Somebody must've heard you telling her."

Tom nodded thoughtfully and narrowed his eyes, making Heck wonder if he'd zeroed in on a suspect. If he had, though, he said nothing.

"Give me a hand fetching the nugget?" Heck asked. "I want

to bring it into the main room so no one knows our hiding spot. You didn't tell Amelia about the hiding spot, did you?"

"No, Heck. I promise."

"You don't have to promise, Tom. You say something, I believe it. I trust you."

Tom looked incredulous. "How could you after this?"

Heck patted his shoulder. "Because you're my brother. You made a mistake. We all make mistakes."

"It was a big mistake."

Heck spread his hands. "You love Amelia and want to be with her. So, if Titus lets you court her, are you really fixing to leave with her in the spring?"

Tom nodded, looking ashamed again.

"Pick your head up, brother. You're a man. You gotta make your own way in the world."

"Yeah, but Mother will be sad."

"She will, but that doesn't change the facts. "You love a girl, you do whatever you have to do to keep her. Come on, let's get that nugget."

CHAPTER 22

Heck laughed at Sam's shocked expression. "Pretty big, huh, Sam?"

"It's… remarkable," the assayer stammered. "Never seen anything like it. I don't know if anyone's ever seen anything like it."

"It makes an impression, that's for sure," Heck said.

Sam nodded, leaning in for a closer look.

"It took my breath away when I first saw it," Hope admitted.

"I still can't breathe right," Sam said. He laid his briefcase on the table. "Won't need that after all."

"What is it?" Mr. Mullen asked.

"Test kit," Sam said distractedly, moving around the table to examine the nugget from various angles. "There's a sort of blowpipe inside and some chemicals. I use it to determine the ratio of gold to ore. But this appears to be solid gold." He lifted his head, and his glowing eyes locked onto Heck. "It's incredible. May I touch it?"

"Sure," Heck said. "Do what you gotta do."

Sam reached out slowly, almost tentatively, and placed a hand on the nugget. He whistled long and low and shook his head. "Most amazing thing I've ever seen. It's solid gold. You said it weighs a hundred pounds?"

"Something like that."

Sam whistled again. "Even at normal rates, you could get sixteen dollars an ounce for this. But this isn't a sack of dust. This is a solid nugget, one of the biggest, best nuggets ever found."

"So what do you think it's worth?" Heck asked.

Sam shrugged. "A nugget like this? I wouldn't be surprised if you could get eighteen or twenty dollars an ounce. Maybe even more."

"Thirty-two thousand dollars?" Hope asked, clearly awed. "Is that much even possible?"

Sam nodded. "There are people out there, Mrs. Martin, with so much money that thirty-two thousand dollars seems a small amount, and some of these people scour the earth for one-of-a-kind items like this nugget. If I could talk to a good lawyer…"

"I'm dealing with a lawyer now. I've never met the guy, but Jim Bridger said he's good, and Jim Bridger's word is bond. This lawyer's taking care of my land claim."

"Good," Sam said, nodding. "It was smart to get that going. How close are you to getting the deed?"

"No idea. I'm sure Jim got right on it, but I don't know how long those things take."

"Hopefully, you'll have the title soon. In the meantime, stake your claim. Put up signs. That way, if anybody comes sniffing around, they'll see it and hopefully keep moving. If word about this nugget gets out, you're going to face an army of prospectors."

Around the room, faces lost their glimmer. It was a daunting notion.

"Is there more gold?" Sam asked.

Heck shrugged. "I've seen a little. But I haven't gone back and looked."

Sam just stared at him for a moment. "You didn't even look?"

"No reason to. Been busy rebuilding the road."

Sam laughed. "No offense, Heck, but you are a strange fellow. Most people would be down there night and day, digging for more gold."

"Yeah, well, the minute a man starts living his life by what most people would do, he's in big trouble," Heck said.

"Here's the thing," Sam said. "Even if you don't find more gold, you might be sitting on the largest gold mine in the world."

"You think?"

"You could be. And that's what makes all the difference. With this nugget as a sample, you could sell this land for an unthinkable sum of money. I can't even imagine how much you might get. Certainly hundreds of thousands of dollars—even if you never find another flake."

Hope's mouth dropped wide open. Her father stepped in and hugged her. Tom's eyes looked like they might pop from his head.

But Heck's own reaction was more akin to that of Mrs. Mullen, whose expression remained wary.

"That's a lot of money," Heck said.

"It sure is," Sam said, "but that's just a minimum. If you find more gold, you might sell this land for millions of dollars, Heck. Millions."

"Huh," Heck said. "That's even more money."

Sam tilted his head and stared at Heck with a confused smile. "I did mention that you're a little on the strange side, didn't I? You don't even sound happy about the news."

"Oh, I'm happy. It's just that we're making out okay right now. I don't want to get carried away, dreaming about money... especially money we don't even need."

"That's wise. But you should at least understand your options. Where is your lawyer?"

"San Francisco."

"When are you going to see him?"

"I hadn't planned on going. Jim was taking care of everything."

"But surely now, considering the nugget, you'll be going," Sam said. "I would be happy to accompany you and speak with the lawyer. I can help him understand this as the artifact it is. That should help him find the right buyer and the right price."

"I appreciate the offer," Heck said, "but here's the thing, Sam. I'm not going anytime soon. I have all the money I need, and if that ever changes, this nugget is a better savings than a stack of coins tucked away in some bank."

"But again, if you sold this land on speculation—"

"I'm not ready to do that," Heck said. "I love this land. And it's not mine to sell, anyway. I would need to talk to Hope and Seeker first."

"Well, not to tell you your business, Heck," Sam said, "but a lot of folks now know about this gold. Most of them are heading west next spring. What do you think the chances are that none of them will speak of this?"

Heck just stared at him. He knew the answer. They all knew the answer.

"I hate to be a doomsayer, Heck," Sam said, "but if you don't do this right, you're going to have a war on your hands."

CHAPTER 23

Heck closed the door of his cabin and sat down at the table with Hope and Seeker.

"Well, what do you think?" he asked.

"I don't really know," Hope said. "On one hand, it's amazing. The type of money Sam's talking about, it doesn't even make sense. Thirty-two thousand dollars? Hundreds of thousands? Millions? We could go back to Kentucky and buy thousands and thousands of acres and build a beautiful home with barns and fences and people to work for us and the fastest quarter horses anyone's ever seen."

"Is that what you want?" Heck asked.

"I don't know what I want anymore," Hope said. "Would I love that life? Sure, though maybe not on such a grand level. I mean, I would enjoy having a nice ranch with a few top horses, but it wouldn't have to be some massive spread. And I'm not sure I'd want to hire our work done, either. I like working."

"So do I," Heck said.

"I know you do, Heck. And that's the other thing. You're sweet to ask what I want, but what about you? I know you love the West."

"I do. I truly do."

"Well then, I wouldn't want to haul you back east. Because I want you to be happy."

"Don't you like it here no more, Hope?" Seeker asked.

"Oh, it's lovely here, Seeker. For now. I just can't help but wonder about what Sam was saying."

"He made some good points. I wish we had the title to the land. In the meantime, I'd best make some signs and hammer them into the borders of our property."

"Does that have any power?" Hope asked. "Legally, I mean."

"If it doesn't, our guns do," Seeker said. "Pa and Ma were the first to settle this land. Ain't no way I'm letting a bunch of greedy prospectors take it."

Heck nodded. "They want war, we'll give them war. I just hope it doesn't come to that."

"This is your home, Seeker," Hope said. "What do you think about selling it?"

Seeker shrugged and avoided her gaze.

"You can say anything," Hope said. "This is your land more than anyone's."

Seeker looked at Hope then at Heck.

Heck nodded. "She's right, little brother."

"Well, she ain't right about this being my land. No offense, Hope. But me and Heck are partners, and partners share everything fifty-fifty. Right, Heck?"

Heck smiled. "That's right, little brother. We're partners till the end."

"So I reckon whatever you want, Heck, we'll do," Seeker said.

Heck could see the boy holding back, so he said, "Partners share everything—including the truth. I appreciate what you're trying to do here, Seeker, but I want to know how you really feel."

The boy shrugged. "I always loved your stories about traveling and seeing the world, and I guess maybe I'd like to do some of that myself, but money just don't seem that important to me is all. I mean, once you got enough, what's the sense in having more?"

Heck nodded, figuring the boy was too young and too inexperienced to understand everything that came into a man's life... but also recognizing the wisdom of Seeker's basic sentiment. Heck figured in a hundred or even two hundred years, folks would probably still be trying to figure out whether money created or cured more problems.

"And, well, if you want the whole of it," Seeker said, "my folks is buried here. I don't want to sell their bones to somebody who might dig 'em up, hunting for gold."

Heck sat back and raised his brows. "Well, there we have it... the absolute truth if I ever heard it. I'm sorry, little brother. That had never even occurred to me. We won't sell an acre of this ground unless you change your mind."

Seeker beamed. "Thanks, Heck. Are you okay with that, Hope?"

"Of course I am, Seeker. Like Heck said, I didn't even think about... you know... your parents."

Heck laid a hand on his wife's shoulder. "Hope, if you ever

decide you want to leave, we'll move. That is my promise to you. And of course, you'll be invited to join us, little brother."

Both Hope and Seeker thanked him.

"Well then," Heck said, "we'll just hope Jim Bridger's lawyer is getting the title arranged. And for the time being, we'll sit on the nugget and hope nobody else finds out about it."

"You don't think anyone will, do you?" Hope said.

"I don't know," Heck said. "But things have dried up pretty good. I expect Burt and his crew will be leaving for Fort Laramie any day now. What are the chances eight men can keep a secret?"

CHAPTER 24

Several days later, after helping to finish the levee, Burt Bickle and his crew were ready to leave for Fort Laramie.

Sam Collins, Abe Zale, Mark Branch, Myles Mason, and Ray McLean were all going with Burt, as were Trace Boon and Jem Pulcher, who'd been lying low since their catastrophic mistake.

"Don't worry, Heck," Sam said while the two of them stood away from the others, "I'll remind everyone not to mention the gold."

"Thanks, Sam. Do what you can do. And stay safe out there."

It was risky, leaving this late in the year, but Burt thought they'd be okay. The men had rifles and food and buffalo robes in case a cold snap hit.

Now, the whole community had turned out to wish them well.

"Should be back in a few weeks if all goes well," Burt said. The muleskinner glowed with purpose as he made one last check of the wagon, gear, and animals.

"You have the list?" Titus asked.

Burt slapped his shirt pocket. "Got it, professor. We'll do our best. At the very least, we'll bring back your wagons—those that'll still roll, that is. If the Injuns burned them, we'll bring back some ashes." He roared with laughter and asked if his crew was ready to depart.

They were.

"One moment, men," Doc said. "Let's all pray for their safe delivery."

Everyone bowed their heads as Doc said, "Father, we thank You for these brave men and ask You to carry them safely to Fort Laramie and home again and that You bless their efforts. In Jesus' name we pray, amen."

"Amen," the community chorused.

Burt and his crew pulled out, and everyone stood in the gate and watched them until they disappeared around the bend.

"Hope they make good time," said Jacob Fox, who'd stuck around to finish the road. "Otherwise, they might get caught in snow."

"Snow," Hope said, holding out her arms and tilting her pretty face toward the sunny sky. "It doesn't even seem possible on a day like today."

"I reckon it'll seem plenty possible to you before long, ma'am," said Amos, who'd trapped beaver in this region. "Winters here tend to make an impression."

"But we're not even close to winter. Not really. It's only October," Hope said.

"Might be October in the rest of the world," Amos said, "but this country doesn't pay attention to calendars. Winter comes when it comes."

"Whatever happens," Heck said, "Burt will get them through. He's a muleskinner to the core. The man bleeds axle grease."

The others nodded, encouraged.

"It's going to seem empty without them here," Sandra Plum said.

"Yeah, especially when it comes time to fill the guard duty roster," A.J. Plum said grimly.

"Do we still need to keep a watch?" Mrs. Plum asked. "We haven't seen a sign of those riders."

"I, for one, think we should maintain the watch," Titus said. "Those riders might have been scouts. If they return with a larger force, we will want advance notice. Otherwise, they might slip over the walls and kill us in our sleep."

Heck nodded. "I happen to agree with Titus. We still have twelve men capable of standing watch," he said, including Seeker and Franky Pillsbury in his count. "I don't need much sleep. I can take a turn every night."

"Likewise," Jacob Fox said.

"I'll stand watch every night so long as I can have first or last shift," A.J. Plum said.

"That'll be between you and Titus," Heck said. "He'll work out the schedules. If anyone else wants to volunteer for extra shifts, let him know."

"I'll stand watch," the Widow said.

"That's all right, ma'am," Titus said. "I'm certain we can manage."

"Nonsense," the Widow snapped. "I'm a good shot and just as steady as any man. I'll do my part. My son will also take a turn standing guard."

Heck turned to the quiet, rail thin boy. "You ready to stay up and guard the fort, Paul?"

The kid's eyes swelled a bit, but he nodded. "Yes, sir."

"Good man," Heck said, patting the kid on the back. Then he turned to the Widow, who wanted nothing more, he knew, than to see her frail, timid son become a capable man. "And thank you, ma'am. That'll help. We need every volunteer we can get."

"I will stand guard as well, Father," Amelia said.

Titus looked shocked. "You?"

"She's of age, Titus," the Widow said with a grin. "It'll do the girl good, and like Heck said, we can use every volunteer we can get."

Titus conceded with a nod, though everyone could see that he wasn't happy with the notion of his lovely daughter standing guard. "Very well, Amelia. I will add you to the schedule."

When they broke apart and went their separate ways, Hope said, "I'm sorry I didn't volunteer to stand guard, Heck. I've just been so tired lately."

"Are you feeling okay otherwise?"

"I'm fine. A little sick here and there but nothing to worry about. I must've eaten something that didn't agree with me. Or maybe it's all the excitement lately. Once I'm feeling like myself again, I'll stand watch, too."

"If you want, but nobody expects you or any other woman to stand guard." He grinned. "The Widow is a breed apart."

"She is. But Amelia also volunteered."

"Yeah, that surprised me."

"Surprised her daddy, too."

"Good," Heck said. "The man needs some surprising. And Hope, do me a favor?"

"Anything, Heck."

"If you keep feeling unwell, talk to Doc about it?"

"Yes, sir," Hope said and saluted him with a smirk on her face. "But don't worry, my love. I'm sure I'm fine."

CHAPTER 25

A week later, beneath a full moon, Amelia stood watch in the guard tower, staring out at the valley as an icy wind stirred the dusting of fresh snow.

As the snow lifted, sparkling in the moonlight, Amelia shivered.

Wrapped in a buffalo robe as she was, the shiver resulted less from the chill of the wind and more from the sounds that wind carried.

Howling.

She'd heard wolves off and on ever since leaving home. Out on the prairie, especially when she'd been new to the trail, the sound had terrified her.

Here in this remote territory, wolves were common. She heard them most nights as they chased their prey or sang their mournful songs.

Behind the walls of the fort, those sounds did little beyond stirring the uncontrollable, primordial loathing she believed natural to all humans. There was something in the howl of a wolf, something primal that made the hairs on one's neck go stiff as pokers.

Oh, Amelia, she laughed to herself, *you certainly do have a straying mind.*

She shivered again as wolves filled the night with their howling.

Something had changed. She'd never heard so many wolves. Not even close.

They had come with the snow. How many, she didn't know, but it seemed they had quadrupled over recent days. Packs sang from all directions, melancholy and foreboding.

Don't worry, she told herself. *You're safe here.*

No sooner had this thought occurred to her than a closer sound that made her grab her father's rifle.

That was no howl.

It had been a voice. A faint, hissing whisper had sliced through the darkness like an arrow.

Indians?

Her heart pounded in her chest as she raised the rifle to her shoulder.

Did they know she was here?

She peered into the moonlit valley beyond the wall but saw no movement save for a feather of sparkling snow that lifted, spun, and fell to the ground as if shot.

What should she do? Call for help? Fire a warning shot?

Then, before she could decide, the voice cut through the night again.

"Amelia," the whisper called from below her, within the compound.

She felt enormous relief. It wasn't Indians. "Who is it?"

"It's me," Tom called, stepping into the moonlight. "Mind if I come up for a visit?"

New fear pierced her heart. Tom wanted to join her here, in the tower, alone, at night?

She had volunteered for this job to show Father she was ready for independence. And yes, part of that had to do with Tom. She'd been frustrated by Father's handling of her courtship.

But independence is not rebellion, and although the idea thrilled her, she did not wish to rebel against her father or her own best interests.

Because if Tom came up here, anything could happen.

"It's the middle of the night, Tom," she said, deflecting his question, not wanting to hurt his feelings.

"I can't sleep. I just lay there, thinking of you. I miss you, Amelia."

"I miss you, too, Tom."

"If that's the case, why have you been avoiding me?"

"I'm not avoiding you, Tom, not really. And certainly not of my choosing. Well, not exactly. It's just… Father."

"Why does he hate me?"

"He doesn't hate you, Tom."

"Why does he look down on me, then?"

And there it was, the crux of the matter, the unfortunate truth… because her Father really did look down on Tom. It was stupid and ugly but true. "He has his ways."

"And you agree with them?"

Suddenly, she felt cross. "Don't pout, Tom. It's not becoming."

"I'm not pouting, Amelia. I'm angry."

"At me?"

"At the situation."

"And Father?"

"Yeah, I guess I'm mad at him, too. He knows about the gold now. So it can't be about money. Why can't I see you?"

"Please keep your voice down, Tom. He hasn't forbidden me from seeing you. That has been my choice."

Tom's mouth went as wide and dark as a grave in the moonlight. "Your choice? But Amelia, I thought…"

"You thought correctly, Tom. I love you, all right? I still love you. And that's exactly why I have been avoiding you lately. It's too painful."

"What do you mean? If you still love me, and your father hasn't forbidden you from seeing me…"

"That's exactly why seeing you is so painful, Tom. Father still insists that we remain friends only."

"But the gold…"

"Be patient, my love. I think in Father's mind, the gold remains somewhat abstract. He's never seen it and knows next to nothing about it, let alone what will become of it."

Tom frowned up at her. "You mean he doesn't think part of it is mine."

"I won't lie to you, Tom. I suspect those are his thoughts. It's terrible, the way he's handling this. I'm sorry. His opinion of you shouldn't hinge solely on money. Besides, you're such a gifted leatherworker and such a hard worker, I'm certain you'll be a wonderful provider for any woman lucky enough to marry you."

"I don't want to marry any woman, Amelia. I want to marry you."

She gasped at his boldness, even as a powerful thrill tickled through her. "Tom, please don't do this to me."

"Let me come up and talk with you, Amelia, please."

"Absolutely not, Tom. If you come up these stairs, I'll never talk to you again. I mean it."

"Don't be angry. I love you, Amelia, that's all, and it's driving me crazy, not being able to see you."

"I love you, too, Tom, and I miss you terribly. But we must be patient."

"I wish I had the money now."

"Forget the money, Tom," Amelia said. "There's nothing you can do about it now. Remain patient and continue being the good man you are. Father will have to notice. And perhaps, when he sees you for who you truly are, he will relent."

Tom stood a little straighter at her charge. "You're right, Amelia. Thank you for helping me see that. I will do whatever it takes to make your father understand that I am the right man for you. Goodnight, my love."

"Goodnight, sweet Tom."

She watched him walk off to his cabin then sat there alone in the tower, adrift in a turbulent sea of love and worry as the wolves howled on and on and on.

CHAPTER 26

Heck and Doc cut across the compound, heading for the stable.

"Where are you two going?" asked Jacob Fox, who'd been talking to the Widow.

"We're going hunting," Heck explained.

Beside him, Doc nodded.

Doc was a great fisherman, but he'd never done much hunting, so Heck knew the man was excited.

Jacob glanced at the sky, where the sun had climbed halfway to its apex already. "Leaving a little late, aren't you?"

"Now that things are warming up, animals will be on the move again," Heck said. "Besides, haven't you heard the wolves lately?"

"I certainly have," the Widow interjected. "I lay awake listening to them."

"Notice how there's more of them?" Heck asked. "They've been coming in from the north."

"Why?" Jacob asked.

"My guess is they're following game. Big herds, I mean."

"Buffalo?" Jacob asked.

"That's right."

"Got room for one more? I've always wanted to shoot a buffalo."

"Sure," Heck said. "Fetch your rifle. We'll wait for you."

As Jacob hurried off, the Widow stepped forward. "Heck, would you be so kind as to take Paul with you?"

Heck hesitated. Many boys hunted well by Paul's age, which Heck estimated to be eleven or twelve; but Paul was so small and timid, he looked about nine, and Heck reckoned the boy would be more trouble than he was worth.

"We've already put up a lot of food, ma'am. I reckon three shooters will bring down enough meat to keep us eating all winter. Paul can stay in school."

"Paul reads and cyphers just fine," the Widow said. "He needs to learn the ways of men more than he needs more schooling. I'm asking you as a favor to take him along."

"You go ahead and fetch him, then, ma'am," Heck said. "We'll be happy to have him along."

The Widow nodded. "Thank you. It was a coughing fever that took my husband. Nigh on three years ago. Paul took sick, too. I was plum worn out, tending to the both of them, worrying, waiting to start coughing myself. I think I was still half asleep, still half dreaming when Paul called to me that night. I remember him rising up in the gloom just as pale as a ghost, saying, 'Mama, Daddy's passed on to the other side.'"

She shook her head as if to clear those thoughts from her mind, but when she spoke again, she continued, "Then Paul—he was just a slip of a boy, you understand, and terribly sick—he set to coughing. I pulled him into my arms and held him and told him not to cry because it would make the coughing worse, but of course he did, we both did. My husband, his father, was a good man, you understand; a righteous man who worked from can to can't day after day with never a cross word for anyone. Paul's coughing did get worse for a time. Then, when it finally stopped, he asked me, *Mama, am I fixing to die, too?"*

Heck swallowed with difficulty, pierced through the heart by the Widow's story. He couldn't help but picture his own father, who'd soldiered on, raising Heck, after Heck's mother had died.

"I told him no, of course," the Widow said. "What else would a mother tell her only child at a time like that? But he certainly seemed to be teetering on death's doorstep. Oh, how I prayed. And I promised the good Lord that if he would just save my Paul, I'd spend the rest of my life trying to see that he grew into a man like his father; a strong, righteous man."

"You're doing an admirable job of that, ma'am," Doc said.

Heck nodded in agreement, words failing him.

"I thank you," the Widow said. "And I will persist in my attempt, which is, after all, nothing less than a covenant with our heavenly Father. He saved my boy, so now it's up to me to raise him up right. But I can't do it alone, gentlemen. I know Paul is small and weak for his age. He never fully regained his strength after the sickness. But I know with your help he can become a good man and can fully recover. I believe that to my core, and that's what I desire above all else, beyond even my own survival. So, you men taking him hunting, well, that means the world to me."

With that, she turned and marched off toward the school, and Heck and Doc, both powerfully affected, merely cleared their throats and continued on to the stable, where Jacob helped them saddle the horses.

A short time later, Paul approached and stopped a short distance away, looking more like a frightened rabbit than a boy. The rifle slung over his shoulder looked too big for him.

Paul stood up straight and said, "Sir, I'd like to go hunting if you'll have me."

Heck stepped forward and shook the boy's hand, looking him in the eyes. "We'll be glad to have you, Paul. And call me Heck. You know Doc and Jacob?"

"Yes, sir… I mean, Heck." Paul stuck out his small hand and shook with the other two men, and together, they brought the horses out and mounted up and rode away from camp into a cool morning that felt warmer for the frigid cold they'd only recently endured.

They headed downstream. When they reached the switch-back trail, Heck said, "Doc, Jacob, why don't you ride along to the new road, and Paul and me will take the old trail."

Jacob grinned. "Don't you trust my engineering knowledge, Heck?"

Heck laughed. "You're the best civil engineer I know, Jacob."

"And the only one you know, I suppose?" Jacob said.

"That's true. But I figured we'll check the old trail for tracks. You boys can do the same while you take the big road."

"Will do, Heck," Doc said. "You keep him out of trouble, Paul."

"Yes, sir," the boy said with a smile.

That was good to see, Heck thought, and he led Paul up the

old switchback trail, moving slowly, checking for tracks and asking Paul to scan their surroundings while he studied the ground in front of them.

"I'll keep an eye out, Heck," Paul said.

The boy's eyes got huge, and it was all Heck could do not to burst out laughing. But he kept it together, and they moved up the twisting trail, Heck looking for signs of intruders and finding nothing, Paul twisting his head from side to side and panning his bulging eyes back and forth like an owl on horseback.

When they topped the ridge, they headed south to meet up with Doc and Jacob.

Halfway there, Paul gasped and pointed up. "What's that, Heck?"

Following the boy's finger, Heck spotted the tawny shape jammed into the notch of a tree ten feet off the ground.

"That, my friend, is a deer."

"What's it doing way up there?"

"Being dead."

"How did it get up the tree?"

"The cougar carried it up there," Heck said.

"A cougar can do that?"

"Cougars are mighty powerful, Paul. They can hold a deer in their mouth and climb right up a tree."

"How come he didn't just eat the deer?"

"I reckon he probably had a meal shortly before he spotted this deer. Put him up there to keep him safe from the wolves and such. Kind of like we store away food for winter."

The boy nodded.

Doc and Jacob came riding up.

"Wondered what happened to you," Jacob said. "What are you looking at? Is that a deer up there?"

"A cougar put it up there," Paul said with enthusiasm.

Doc shuddered. "Now, that's just creepy. Let's get out of here and go buffalo hunting."

They rode south across the ridge, taking their time and following game trails through the forest, Heck pointing out to Paul where different things had happened. Normally, while hunting, he wouldn't make so much noise, but if buffalo had indeed moved into the region, they wouldn't be in the woods, they'd be down in the lush grass of the valleys south of here.

Besides, buffalo had almost no fear of mankind, let alone the noises he made. If they were grazing, you could shoot a buffalo, and the others wouldn't even run off.

The ridge bent and broke apart, the western portion angling off to scale another peak while the eastern section descended toward the grassy valley.

Riding down this slope with their rifles at the ready, they peered out through the mostly leafless trees and beheld an amazing sight: thousands of buffalo grazing in the tall grasses.

Glancing at a clearly amazed Paul, Heck nudged the boy's shoulder and whispered, "What do you think of that, Paul?"

"There's so many of them."

"There must be a thousand," Doc said, looking just as amazed as the boy.

"A few thousand at least, I'd reckon," Heck said. "And if my guess is right, there will be even more in the next valley. I think they came through west of here, hooked into that valley to the south, and are just pushing into this one."

"Whatever the case, I hereby stake a claim on the buffalo hump," Jacob said with a grin.

"There'll be plenty for all of us," Heck chuckled.

"Spoken like a man who's never seen me wrangle a buffalo hump," Jacob said, and they reached the bottom of the hill and rode out of the woods just as four Indians rode into view, coming over a knoll fifty yards away.

CHAPTER 27

Both parties reined in, seeing each other at the same time.

In that moment, the world slowed for Heck as it always did when his life was on the line—as it was now, he realized, seeing the hard faces and ready rifles of the men and faded, blood-stained blue jacket of the middle rider. With uncanny speed, Heck's mind noted the bullet holes in what he recognized as the coat of a United States soldier this Indian had killed. In that same instant, he realized the other Indians were wearing similar battle badges: tall boots, stained handkerchiefs, a battered cavalry hat…

For half a second, the two groups stared at one another, the air crackling with that strange energy that precedes abrupt and cataclysmic violence.

Heck recognized that energy, as did the man in the blue coat, he saw.

Who moved first, Heck couldn't say.

A second later, the air crashed with gunfire, both parties firing simultaneously.

Heck felt a bullet whiz past his head and at the same time saw his target—the leader in the blue coat—hunch unnaturally then drop from his horse.

The air was full of shouting and screaming and gun smoke.

Heck spurred Red and raced forward at an angle, not wanting to provide an easy target and needing to get closer. He leaned over the stallion, who thrummed beneath him, loving combat as always. Heck shoved his Hawken into its scabbard and pulled his Colt and wheeled sharply into the Indians' left flank.

One startled warrior turned and fired, and Heck felt the tug of the bullet pluck against the sleeve of his buckskin jacket as he leveled his own pistol and pulled the trigger, timing Red's rhythm.

The Indian who'd nearly killed him went down in a heap.

Heck pulled back the hammer and fired again, then pulled it back and fired again, then pulled it back... but there was no one left to kill.

Across the way, someone was down. Another man crouched over him. And there, sitting on his horse, was Paul.

The boy's face was bloody and pale, and he blinked ahead as if trapped in a dream. "Everyone okay?" Heck called, knowing they weren't.

Doc turned back and shook his head. "Jacob's dead, Heck. There's nothing I can do for him."

Paul retched then wiped at his mouth and said, "I killed an Indian, Heck. He shot at me, and I shot at him, and I saw his head jerk back, and he fell off his horse. That's him there."

Heck looked down and saw an Indian who'd been shot right between the eyes. "Good job, Paul. You probably saved a life today."

He said this though he knew it wasn't true. The Indian never would have reloaded before Heck would've shot him dead with the Colt.

But Paul didn't need to know that. Paul needed to understand that he'd stood strong and done proud by his mother, killing the way men sometimes were forced to kill on the frontier.

It was a waste. The whole thing was a miserable waste.

And now Jacob, a man Heck had come to think of as a friend, was dead.

Well, there was nothing they could do to change that now. Heck knew as a veteran of many such engagements, there was nothing they could do but take him back and give him a proper burial.

Now, it was time to deal with the living.

Heck hopped down and made sure the Indians were dead.

Based on their white-painted pompadours, double braids, and intricate beadwork, Heck judged these men as members of the Crow tribe.

Were they ranging on their own, or were they part of a larger band?

There was no way to tell. Even though these men fit the tracks they'd seen crossing the ridge, that didn't mean they weren't a detachment of scouts from a larger group that rode a different route.

Heck gathered their horses and rifles and checked their bags and clothing, coming up with a handy little derringer, a fair amount of shot and powder, a few gold coins, and a good supply of pemmican and prairie turnips.

He reckoned they had a camp nearby. They would have more meat there. Perhaps even a good deal of meat and maybe other items of value.

But there are also might be dozens of Indians there, too, so Heck figured they'd just quit while they were ahead.

He led the horses back to his friends.

Paul had dismounted. Doc was using one hand to press a bloody handkerchief to the side of Paul's head.

Meanwhile, Doc was packing his other arm close to his body, and Heck could tell he was hurting. But he was pushing through the pain and taking care of the boy.

"Paul, you are going to have an interesting scar on the side of your head," Doc said. "For the rest of your life, folks will ask about it, and you'll be able to tell them about the time you went to war with some Indians."

"Am I hit bad?" the boy asked.

"Nah, you'll live," Doc said with a smile, but as Doc shifted for a better look, Heck saw his friend wince.

"You shot?" Heck asked.

Doc nodded. "In and out. I'll be all right. What really hurts is this." He turned and half-lifted his arm. The wrist was clearly broken. "Bullet hit me low in the side just as I was firing. Next thing I knew, I was on the ground. Felt my arm break. Grabbed my rifle, but I couldn't even hold it with my bad arm. Couldn't even reload."

"I still reckon we got off easy," Heck said. "Those men were warriors."

"It was a terrifying moment, not being able to reload," Doc

confessed. "If you weren't here, Heck, I'd be dead. You, too, Paul. Thank you."

Paul offered a weak smile. "I killed him, didn't I, Heck?"

"You sure did, Paul."

The boy retched again then apologized.

"You got nothing to be sorry about, son," Heck said. "Killing a man is bad business. Sometimes, like today, you can't help it. But it's never easy." He laid a hand on the boy's shoulder.

Paul was trembling badly.

Heck stared into his eyes. "You did what you had to do, Paul. You stayed calm even when the lead was flying, even when your enemy shot you in the head. I'm proud of you. And I know if your daddy was here, he'd be proud of you, too."

It was too much for Paul, who finally broke. With a desperate cry, he threw his arms around Heck and sobbed. Heck comforted the boy as best he could, returning his embrace while still twisting his head around to make sure no other riders showed up.

None did. But that didn't mean some wouldn't.

He gave Paul a minute then said, "Well, we'd best get on out of here in case more of them are fixing to show up."

"Do you think more will come?" Doc asked.

"I doubt it, but I'd rather not stick around to make sure. I'll load Jacob onto his horse then get the trail ropes hitched, and we'll head back. You need a hand getting back up, Doc?"

"Would you mind?"

"Not at all, my friend. Paul, reload your gun, then reload Doc's and Jacob's. Can you do that?"

"Yes, sir."

Heck grinned. "Hey, what did I tell you about that sir stuff?"

"I'll do it, Heck."

"Good man. And Paul? When you're reloading Doc's gun and Jacob's, make sure the hammers are down and there's no mud in the barrel. You don't want to go tamping dirt into the works."

"All right, Heck."

It took a while, but they got everything together and rode back up the ridge, trailing the extra horses.

They had lost a good man and come away with no meat to speak of, and Doc's arm was in bad shape, but the day hadn't been a total loss.

The extra rifles and horses were valuable, and it was good to know that they had eliminated four clearly hostile men from their territory, but more importantly, they had stood in the face of deadly action.

For Heck, this was nothing new, but Doc and Paul would be changed forever.

Did it make up for the loss of Jacob?

No, not even close.

But Heck's familiarity with death allowed him to remain pragmatic.

And on the frontier, survival wasn't merely about surviving skirmishes. It was how those terrible moments changed and strengthened you.

CHAPTER 28

"Jacob was a good man," Heck said, when it was his turn to speak over the fresh grave, which they had placed on a bank across the river, figuring it would be the best spot for a cemetery should a town really crop up here.

"He had a good attitude and a good mind," Heck continued, "and I was looking forward to having him as a neighbor. We couldn't have built the levee without him. But now he's gone."

He paused, letting the grim assembly dwell on that truth for a moment. There were some tears but mostly just long faces. Jacob was well liked, but most of these folks had lost friends or family along the way.

"His death should be a reminder of how quickly any one of us might meet our end. We didn't do anything wrong. We just went riding out of the woods, and there they were. Those Indians were as surprised as we were. Then the bullets were flying. And that was that. One moment, Jacob was alive. The next, he wasn't. It's a reminder, folks. In the wilderness, death is always close. We can't fear that, but we can't ignore it, either. We have to stay alert and make our peace with the persistent dangers of this life."

People nodded, recognizing the truth.

Beside Heck, Hope wept. That surprised him, as she'd never been particularly close to Jacob.

But of course, Heck understood his own reactions to death weren't exactly normal. He'd seen much death and dealt a good deal of it. That part of him had calloused over to a degree. He would miss Jacob. He wished Jacob was still alive. But crying for him wouldn't do any good.

He draped an arm over Hope's shaking shoulders and comforted her as others spoke, recounting moments they'd enjoyed with Jacob.

Then Doc led them in prayer. Earlier, he'd cleaned and bandaged his gunshot wound and Paul's, and with the help of Heck and Veronica Pillsbury, the midwife, he managed to splint and wrap his broken arm.

If Doc was in pain—and Heck was sure he was hurting bad —he didn't show it. He said the words, and they filled the grave, fixed the marker, and crossed the river in silence.

The Widow, Heck noticed, walked beside her son with her chin in the air. If you didn't know her, you might have mistaken her expression for one of pride.

Heck suspected she was struggling with grief and gratitude and the terror of how close her only son, her only remaining family, had come to dying—on an excursion she had arranged, no less.

But she was a strong woman and wise, too, and she did hold it together. If she wanted this experience to strengthen

Paul, she couldn't coddle him or show any weakness on her part.

Heck admired her.

Hope, still sniffling, retreated into the cabin.

Heck was about to join her when Seeker caught up to him.

"I sure do wish I had ridden with you," Seeker said as they reentered the fort.

"We could've used you, little brother, but it's okay. We got the job done."

"Still, I feel like I let you down."

"Let me down? Not even close. We went out to shoot some buffalo and bumped right into those Indians. If I'd known that was gonna happen, I would've brought everybody and their rifles, but there was no way to see that coming."

"Yeah, but still…"

"Still nothing. If you'd been there, Jacob would still be dead. We all fired at the same time, them and us. Another rifle would've ended things a little faster, but it wouldn't have saved Jacob."

"All right, but next time, I'm riding with you."

"Don't start thinking that way, little brother. You're doing a good job with school."

"Yeah, but—"

"Hear me out," Heck insisted. "This place is dangerous. Death can come at anytime. You know that better than anyone."

Seeker nodded.

"But that doesn't mean you gotta stick right at my side. I can handle myself. And you can handle yourself. If we want to make our home here, we gotta accept some risk. Trick is to stay ready but keep on living our lives."

"So you really think I should keep going to school?"

"I do. You're doing a good job, Seeker. I can't believe how quick you're learning. I'm proud of you."

"Thanks, Heck. Did Paul really kill one of the Indians?"

"He did."

Seeker glanced over to where Paul, now surrounded by children, was no doubt telling his version of the story again—a thing Heck was certain he would do dozens of times in the coming days.

The boy had already changed. He stood straighter and looked anything but timid. His face was animated as he told the story, jerking his head and firing an invisible rifle.

Little Elizabeth Pillsbury pointed up at the bandage, probably wanting to see the gunshot wound on the side of his temple.

Paul shook his head.

Elizabeth did not persist. After all, Paul had new status among the children.

"I'm glad," Seeker said. "We need another steady hand, especially with so many men out on the trail."

"That's right. Maybe you could teach him a thing or two."

"Maybe," Seeker said. "I don't really know him. He's good at reading and math. I'll get him away from them kids and talk to him."

"Sounds good, little brother. Make sure he knows how to clean and handle the Indian rifle."

"All right. You give it to him?"

"He killed the man. It's his. Teach him how to care for that paint pony, too, would you?"

"Sure thing, Heck."

Heck went into his cabin and found Hope on the bed, sobbing.

It shocked Heck. He went to her. "Are you okay?"

She was crying too hard to respond.

He held her and rubbed her back and waited.

Finally, her sobbing subsided, and she blinked up at him with puffy eyes. "I'm sorry, Heck."

"For what?"

"For falling apart like that," she said. "I don't know what's wrong with me. I just couldn't stop crying."

"It's okay, Hope. Really. It's sad. He was a good man."

She nodded. "He was. But I wasn't crying for him. I was crying for you."

"Me? I didn't even get scratched."

"Not this time. I'm so scared of losing you, Heck."

"Well, you know how it goes, Hope. I'll do my best to survive. I'm pretty good at it."

She nodded and started crying again. It didn't last so long this time.

"I praise God that you're safe," she said. "I know I shouldn't worry. I know God doesn't want me to worry, and I know worrying doesn't help you at all, but I just can't help it."

"I didn't know you worried much."

"That's the thing. I didn't use to. It's just over recent weeks. It's like I'm a different person. More emotional, almost fragile. And I hate it."

"Don't be too hard on yourself," Heck said. "Things like this come and go. You'll be back to normal in no time."

They embraced.

Then a knock came at the door. A voice cried out.

Uh oh, Heck thought. *Are we under attack? Were there more Crow warriors?*

But when he opened the door, he saw the cry was not someone sounding the alarm but rather Susan Haines yelping on tiptoes.

Her older sister had her by the ear.

Looking furious, Amelia demanded, "Tell him, Susan."

"I'm sorry, Mr. Martin," Susan wept. "It was me."

"What do you mean?" Heck said.

"Tell him," Amelia growled.

"It was me," Susan said again. She wouldn't meet his eyes. "I'm the one who told."

"Told what?" Heck said.

"About the gold," Susan said. "I heard Tom tell Amelia and then… well… I'm sorry, Heck."

She started crying again.

Heck put a hand on her shoulder. "I wish you hadn't done that, Susan, but thank you for telling me."

The girl lifted her eyes, and they were full of fear. "I'm so sorry, Mr. Martin. You won't kick me out, will you?"

"Kick you out?" Heck laughed. "No. Not ever. Look, if I kicked anyone out, it'd be the men who broke into my cabin looking for the gold, or maybe Tom for spilling the beans in the first place. You shouldn't have done what you did, but I reckon you know that now, don't you?"

She nodded solemnly. "I do, Mr. Martin. I really do. I'm awful sorry."

He could see she meant it. "I forgive you, Susan. You're a good girl. I'm happy you're here with us."

"Thank you, Mr. Martin. Thank you so much."

CHAPTER 29

With each passing day, the weather seemed to move in reverse, growing more lovely. Three days after the mix-up with the Indians, the valley was full of sunshine and birdsong. It felt like mid-July.

"Well, praise God for this unexpected surprise," Hope said that morning when Heck, returning from the hole downstream with two nice trout, commented on the gorgeous weather. "In light of this beautiful day, would you do me a favor, Mr. Martin?"

"My answer remains the same as always, Mrs. Martin. You want something, all you gotta do is ask. I'll do anything for you."

"Take me on a picnic."

"A picnic?"

"Take me someplace for lunch. Just the two of us."

"What, today? I told A.J. Plum I'd—"

"Well, whatever you were going to do, tell Mr. Plum you'll help him later. How often do I interrupt your days?"

"Never."

"That's right. Please, Heck? Winter's just around the corner. I'd love to take a picnic together and enjoy this beautiful weather."

He smiled. "Okay. I'll tell Plum."

"Thank you." She kissed him. "I know just where I want to take the picnic."

"You've really thought this out, huh?"

She nodded. "I've already packed sandwiches and apples and a blanket for us to sit on."

He laughed. "Like a fancy lord and lady."

"For today, yes. Then we'll be back to regular old Heck and Hope tomorrow. Now, are you going to let me tell you where I want to eat, or will you persist in interrupting me?" she joked.

"Do tell. I'm dying to know."

"You know the hidden valley?"

"The one you and Tom discovered where the caves open up on top of the ridge?"

"Right. That's where I want to go."

"All right. We can do that. Just let me go tell Plum, and I'll be back in a moment." He opened the door, then paused there, shaking his head and grinning. "Prepare your picnic, m'lady."

An hour later, they entered the magical valley by way of the caves. The beautiful day was magnified here because the canyon atop the ridge, open to the sky, held the heat. Birds sang pleasantly. Wispy white clouds drifted slowly across the bright blue sky, and their reflections followed suit, sailing across the surface of the little pond at the center of the hidden valley.

"I shouldn't have made fun of your idea," Heck said as they spread the blanket beside the shimmering pool. "This is nice."

"It sure is. I'll cherish this memory all through the winter."

He kissed her. "Me, too."

Then, suddenly, Hope was weeping again.

"What is it?" Heck asked, confused.

She smiled at him through her tears. "You're going to be a father."

Heck opened his mouth, but no words came out.

Hope laughed.

Heck finally found his voice. "You mean...?"

Hope nodded. "I'm pregnant, Heck. We're going to have a baby."

A torrent of emotions flooded him: excitement, wonder, joy, trepidation, gratitude, and above all else, love. "A baby..."

"That's right. And you're going to be the best father in the world. But don't tell Daddy I said that."

"Oh, Hope, this is wonderful news," Heck said, and hauled her into his arms.

They kissed and held their embrace for a long time, expressing their love and excitement and wondering aloud what it would be like, having a child, and exactly who that little person would end up being.

"I hope it's a girl," Heck said, "and I hope she's just like you."

Hope shook her head. "It will be a boy. Trust me."

"How do you know?"

"I just know. We're going to have a son, and I pray that he is as strong and kind and decent as his father."

CHAPTER 30

One frigid afternoon three weeks later, Burt Bickle's crew returned.

Folks shouted and cheered as the wagons rolled triumphantly through the gate, accompanied by a wonderful surprise… far more livestock than Heck could have hoped for— not just mules, horses, and cattle but also oxen, goats, sheep, and pigs.

The lead wagon came to a halt. Burt stood and addressed everyone, beaming like a politician. "Bickle Freighting finds a way, ladies and gentlemen!"

They roared their appreciation, spreading out, different groups hurrying to specific wagons.

This was the moment they had been dreaming of. Their wagons and possessions had been returned to them.

The wagon men were hauled from their perches, embraced, and clapped on the back, everyone shouting their joyous thanks. Families crawled into their wagons and celebrated together as they discovered items they'd thought lost forever.

Heck approached Burt, who shook his hand and puffed out his chest, proud as a peacock.

"Nice work, Burt."

"Thanks, Heck. Told you we'd find a way."

Noticing bullet holes and broken-off arrows peppering Burt's wagon, Heck said, "Run into Indian trouble?"

"On the way there, yeah, but we made it through."

"How did you get so much stock?"

"These animals are trail-broke. Once you feed 'em and lead 'em to water, they'll follow you through whatever the trail throws at you: rain, mud, snow, doesn't matter."

"That's great," Heck said. "But I'm surprised the soldiers parted with so many, what with winter coming on."

"That's all because of you, Heck," Burt said.

"Me? I didn't do anything."

"Oh yes, you did. A couple of years ago, you apparently saved a struggling supply officer at Fort Bent. They were running low on meat, and you went out and hunted for them, even with a big storm coming in."

Heck grinned at that. "You ran into Captain Scottsdale?"

"It's Major Scottsdale now, and he's head of supply at Fort Laramie. He was a pretty gruff fellow when we first tried buying stock."

Heck laughed. "Yeah, Scottsdale drives a tough bargain."

"Tough? That ain't the half of it. Said he wouldn't sell us so much as a solitary chicken. But then he heard your name, and everything changed."

"He's a good man."

"He said the same thing about you. Had a million questions about you, what you've been up to, what you were planning to do. Wanted to know every little detail. But the important thing is, as soon as he knew we were with you, everything changed. They put us up, free of charge, fed us hot meals, then parted with all this stock you see here and a few others that were lost along the way."

"Well, I'll have to thank him the next time I see him."

"That's not all," Burt said. "Major Scottsdale, knowing we'd run into some trouble along the way, escorted us through the worst Indian territory. He and his men rode a hundred miles or more. Then, once he reckoned we were safe, he turned them around and headed back for Laramie."

"That was mighty kind of him," Heck said.

"Sure was," Burt said, "and here." He reached into his pocket, pulled out an envelope, and handed it to Heck. "He wanted me to give this to you."

"Thanks," Heck said, and opened the letter. Inside, neat handwriting read:

DEAR HECK,

WELL, OLD FRIEND, IT SOUNDS LIKE YOU'RE MAKING YOUR MARK ON *the world.*

I'm not surprised. You always were a breed apart.

I hope the livestock help you establish Fort Seeker and Heck's Valley. They're good animals. If you can keep from slaughtering over the winter, you will really have something come next year.

I will do my best to visit in the spring. Official business, of course. What kind of cavalry supply officer wouldn't familiarize himself with a new trading post along the way?

The colonel doesn't need to know I'm mainly visiting in hopes of getting my revenge on the chess board.

It's good to be back in the same territory with you, Heck. I'm confident Fort Seeker will be a powerful stabilizing force in the region.

YOUR FAITHFUL FRIEND,
Major Avery Scottsdale

P.S. I'VE SENT ALONG SOMETHING FOR YOU. ACCORDING TO YOUR friend, you already have a private library, but knowing how quickly you read, you've probably already read and reread everything. Enjoy.

HECK LOOKED UP FROM THE LETTER, AND BURT WAS HOLDING the book out to him.

Heck took it and read the cover aloud. *"The Scarlet Letter* by Nathaniel Hawthorne. Well, that was mighty nice of the good major."

CHAPTER 31

A few inches of snow fell and didn't melt. Temperatures had dropped below freezing and seemed reluctant to rise above that point.

Luckily, the animals could still forage in the pasture.

Wild game had practically disappeared, and one gloomy afternoon, a large mountain lion drifted off the wooded slope as silently as a tawny ghost and attacked a goat.

The predator was so stealthy and fast there was no chance of saving the goat, but a second later, a rifle shot cracked, the cougar was no more, and eleven-year-old Paul Wolfe, who'd been watching the herd, had cemented his status among the children as a man in the making.

Heck was one of the first to reach the boy. He congratulated Paul and told him to take the goat home to his mother.

Meanwhile, Heck was pleased by the prospect of cougar meat. Folks who'd never had it were always dubious, but mountain men loved cougar the way Apaches loved mule.

With winter upon them, folks were glad they had stored plenty of food and firewood. Because of the stream running through the caves, water would never be a problem, even when the temperatures dropped below zero and the river outside froze solid.

There was still work to be done, of course, but with winter, there was also time for leisure.

Women had time to gossip, fix inventive meals, and play games with their children.

Men had time to spend with their families and tell stories and plan for spring. They wondered if the levee would hold against the spring flood and if they would hold against spring raiders.

Evenings were full of music, storytelling, and the laughter of children.

Friendships deepened.

Meanwhile, Hope glowed with happiness and good health. She was beginning to show. When she at last confessed her condition to her family, Mr. and Mrs. Mullen were elated.

Mr. Mullen pulled Heck into a powerful embrace and slapped him on the back. "Oh, Heck, my boy! You've made me the happiest man alive!"

Mrs. Mullen cried tears of joy—a thing Heck never thought he'd see—and Tom pumped Heck's hand up and down, congratulating him over and over.

"I guess I really am gonna be an uncle," Seeker said, beaming like he'd just been named King of the Wilderness. "Huh. Me, an uncle…"

A short time later, they shared the happy news with the community at large and received another wave of warmth and enthusiasm. Folks were overjoyed to know Heck's Valley would soon see the birth of its first baby.

After more snow fell, Heck spent a good deal of time exploring the caves. He spent some of that time looking for gold and did find more flakes and nuggets, the largest of which was about the size of his thumb. Mostly, however, he explored the other passageways and caverns, which seemed to go on forever.

Seeker usually accompanied him and started drawing maps of the cave complex. This slowed their progress, but Heck was impressed by the boy's skill and knew a map would come in handy.

When Heck and Seeker weren't exploring the subterranean wonderland, they spent a lot of time snowshoeing the surrounding territory. During these excursions, they sometimes visited Black Cloud, who frequently joined them.

The Shoshone understood, as Heck understood, that a man must know the land around his home. A man must commit everything to memory. Such knowledge could mean the difference between life and death if he is injured or caught out during bad weather.

As they explored, they named various features.

So now, when someone referred to the Johnson Woods, they knew it meant where Amos Johnson had been attacked by the bear. Just as Johnson Rock was the cluster of rocks where Heck had first found Amos.

There was Hope Falls, where Hope had leapt off the ridge into what was now known as the Big Hole for the depth and width of that river section.

Other names—like the Big Oak, the Salt Lick, the Mossy

Bank, and the Middle Woods—were purely pragmatic but no less useful.

These shared names would allow the citizens of Heck's Valley to communicate while hunting together or defending their homes.

Then, suddenly, it was Christmas Eve. Doc, whose arm was healing nicely, led a service celebrating the birth of their Lord and Savior, Jesus Christ. There was singing and much merriment and gratitude.

Overnight, more snow fell, and families mostly stuck to their cabins until midday, when they came together to enjoy a Christmas feast hosted by the Mullens. It was a glorious celebration with bread and soup, mashed potatoes and carrots, and beef from one of the steers Burt had brought back from Laramie.

Heck, who hadn't had beef in what felt like years, decided right on the spot that he was going to bring more cattle into the valley.

Afterward, there was music and games, singing and dancing. Everyone was dazzled by the fine dancing of Tom and Amelia— everyone, that was, except Titus, who frowned as his daughter spun and laughed and curtseyed.

Then the women unveiled the desserts they'd spent so long preparing for this most special occasion.

Hope's pumpkin pie was so good Heck had a second piece.

It was a wonderful day, and Heck was very thankful for his friends and family, especially his lovely wife and the baby he couldn't wait to meet.

Then Christmas was over, and winter stretched on, giving folks time to think and dream and make decisions.

Three of the bachelors—Trace Boon, Jem Pulcher, and Mark Branch—grew restless and talked frequently of spring, when they would finally be able to restart their westward journey.

Amos Johnson announced he would also be leaving. "I'm healed up now, and my bones are aching with the need to see the far places. It's who I am, Heck. Just a wandering soul, chronicling the deeds of great frontiersmen."

But not everyone was still dreaming of the West Coast.

Myles Mason, who seemed to have contracted the entrepreneurial spirit of Burt Bickle and Abe Zale, now spoke of helping to build the town and starting a furniture and under-taker business.

And Ray McLean, who seemed always to be fixing some-thing or working out a creative solution for one of the many problems that invariably arose in frontier life, sometimes talked of staying on, too.

Heck hoped he would. Myles, too. He liked them, and they were both highly valuable to the community.

A.J. Plum had also decided to stay on and frequently wandered out of the gate to stand on the spot where he wanted to put his shop and home. Plum could be irritable and severe, but he was a good man, trustworthy and hardworking, and quite talented at the forge.

Both Pillsbury families also decided to stay.

This pleased Hope, who would need a midwife come June.

"I can really see it now," Hope said one evening when she and Heck retreated to their cabin.

"See what?"

"The town."

"What town?"

"This town, the town we could become. People are coming together. And that's what a town is: not buildings and businesses. People."

"Never thought about it like that, but I reckon you're right."

"If these people come together, they'll make it," she said. "They'll build something. They'll create a town that can last. I think these people are up to it. Then, next summer, when the emigrants start rolling through, I think we'll pull together even more."

"You might be right, Hope."

She nodded. "They'll feel pride and kinship. Ownership, even."

"I can see that. And when other people ask to join, well, that'll just make these folks even prouder to be founding members."

"What will we call it?"

"Fort Seeker, I guess."

"The whole town?"

"You have a better idea?"

Hope shook her head. "Fort Seeker is a great name for the fort, but maybe someone will come up with a town name that really expresses how we feel here."

Overall, it was a cozy winter, and folks grew closer.

Then, in late January, trouble hit.

CHAPTER 32

One curiously calm day, with the temperatures hovering just above freezing, a strange cloud appeared to the north. It looked like a gray wall moving slowly and steadily southward, toward them.

The animals grew agitated, and birds filled the sky, chittering anxiously as they hurtled away from the advancing wall.

Heck didn't like the look of it. But he also figured if there was one time that he'd catch game out and about, this was it.

So he grabbed his rifle and fetched Red and headed up to the ridge. Tom went with him.

Heck's theory proved to be correct, and less than an hour after leaving, they were gutting a nice, fat doe. It was exciting because they hadn't had fresh meat since the Christmas steer, but their excitement was dampened by the arrival of wet, heavy flakes that soon crystallized as the wind picked up and the temperature plummeted sharply.

"We'd best be getting back," Tom said.

"You're right," Heck said. "I don't like the looks of this storm. Feels like we're about to get walloped. We gotta get the cows in."

By the time they reached the pasture, several inches of new snow already lay on the ground.

The cattle lay back in the pines, sheltering against the storm. It took some doing, but Heck and Tom got them up and pushed them toward home.

By the time he got the cattle in and returned Red to the stable and cared for him and hung up the quartered meat, the wind was whipping, and it was snowing so heavily Heck could no longer make out the surrounding mountains.

Heck staggered through the snow, looking forward to getting inside his warm cabin. "Come on in," he hollered to Tom over the strengthening wind. "Your sister will have a pot of coffee ready."

Sure enough, Hope met them at the door with a steaming mug of coffee. Seeing Tom, she went to fetch another cup, calling over her shoulder, "Are you two all right?"

"Yeah," Heck said. "Storm surprised us. Came out of nowhere."

"Sure did," Tom agreed. "I'm half frozen."

"We got the cattle in and the meat hung up, anyway," Heck said, sipping the good, hot coffee.

"Oh, you got fresh meat?" Hope said, sounding excited as she carried Tom's mug to him.

Outside, the wind howled like a banshee.

But here in the cabin, the warmth, the good smells of food

cooking, and the pleasure of seeing Hope all conspired to make Heck very happy.

Then someone was hammering on the door.

Heck opened it to reveal the terrified face of Titus Haines. "The children are lost in the storm. I released them early from school, but instead of heading straight home, they went out of the fort to play. Susan is with them. I had no idea... I never would have..."

"We gotta go get them before it's too late," Heck told Tom, who nodded and put down his coffee.

"I'll need my buffalo coat," Titus said, misunderstanding.

"You stay here and tell the parents what's happening," Heck said. "They probably think the kids are still with you. But don't let any of the parents come out to help us. This is a blizzard. It's already bad out there. Before long, you won't be able to see six inches in front of you. Tom and I will do our best to find the kids and bring them home, but we won't have time to go searching for lost adults, too."

Titus started to protest, but Heck cut him off. "I don't have time to argue. More to the point, those kids don't have time. Stay strong, Titus. Don't let those parents give you any grief. This is the only way."

Heck and Tom went back out into the storm. Everything was blinding white. The temperature had dropped another ten degrees, and the wind wailed, scouring their exposed faces with gritty snow that stung the skin like shards of glass.

The storm had escalated into a a full-blown blizzard.

Where were those kids?

Any tracks were long ago wiped out.

He hoped they had holed up somewhere. Otherwise, they wouldn't last long.

Heck frowned, knowing what he had to do. Concern for the children chilled him to his core.

They trudged beyond the gate. Everything was white. Everything was the same.

"This way!" Tom shouted over the screaming wind. "They usually play over here."

"Lead the way!" Heck shouted. He followed his brother-in-law, squinting and shuffling forward, trying to keep the location of Fort Seeker clear in his mind.

One quick glance over his shoulder confirmed his suspicions. The fort was completely invisible now, wrapped in a swirling shroud of white.

The fierce, frigid wind stole his breath and froze his beard.

Heck stayed right behind Tom. If they drifted apart, there would be no way to find one another again and no way for either of them to see even their own tracks in the snow.

Tom stopped and shouted.

Heck leaned close, trying to untangle his brother-in-law's words from the roar of the blizzard.

"...should be close," Tom hollered. "Counted my steps."

"We gotta find these kids soon, or they're gonna die!'

They staggered forward, gripping each other's arms, calling out occasionally into the swirling void of snowy oblivion.

Then, Heck spotted a faint brightness through the snow.

"Fire!" he told Tom, and they were just starting toward it when a weak cry sounded in the other direction. "Must be the kids split up and got trapped apart by the storm!"

"You go to the fire!" Tom shouted. "I'll go to the voice! Meet back at the fort!"

"You have your bearings?"

"I'll be okay, Heck! Let's save these kids!"

With no further ado, they parted ways—for what Heck knew might be the last time.

CHAPTER 33

A short time later, Heck followed the weak illumination to where several children huddled beside a fire just inside the forest. The fire would have gone out, but it had been built—hastily, no doubt—in the lee of the great roots of a fallen tree, and someone had piled branches and snow to make a second wind wall and a makeshift reflector.

Given the circumstances, it was nothing short of brilliant.

Then, reaching them, Heck spotted the source of that brilliance.

"I'm glad to see you, big brother!" Seeker shouted.

Behind him, several children, none of them dressed for the surprise storm, huddled miserably together, their small faces twisted with astonishment, discomfort, and desperation.

"We have to go back now!" Heck shouted. "We must stay together! If any one gets lost, he'll die!"

Little Martina Plum wore only a thin jacket and could

JOHN DEACON

barely move. Heck picked her up and wrapped his coat around her. "Hold on, baby girl. I'll get you home."

The children gathered close to him.

"We will travel single file," Heck told them in a loud voice. "I will take the front. Seeker, you take the back. Everybody, hold onto the belt or coat of the person in front of you. Otherwise, you will get lost in the storm and die."

The children nodded and arranged themselves in a single file.

"Let's go," Heck said, and wondering how Tom was faring, he strode into the white death.

Heck and the children trudged through the snow with torturous slowness.

Howling down the canyon out of the north, its ferocity unbroken by trees or stones or structures, the fearsome blizzard sliced their flesh with its icy grit.

The cold pressed in from all directions like a hungry wolf looking for a way to steal the warmth of these struggling, living things. It pushed through Heck's warm clothing and slipped into the slightest openings, chilling his blood.

He couldn't imagine how the children were suffering. There was nothing he could do except save as many of them as possible.

Even then, he had no idea how many were still with him. He held tight to little Martina and plodded slowly forward, thankful to feel the hand of Martin Plum still holding onto him from behind.

Battered by the ravenous wind, they stumbled through a swirling world of biting cold and blinding whiteness, Heck hoping beyond all hope that his sense of direction remained true even under these terrible conditions.

With excruciating slowness, they plodded forward, stopping frequently as children slipped and fell.

Heck kept putting one foot in front of the other and struggled through the knifelike wind and constant white wall of sleet and snow, praying for deliverance.

But then, all of a sudden, he bumped into the palisade.

Greatly encouraged, he shouted back to the children. "We're almost home! Hold tight!"

When they reached his cabin and opened the door, Heck had never been so happy to see home—any home—in all his life.

The children stumbled inside, stunned and weeping and shivering, to be snatched up by parents waiting there for them, while the warmth of the space enveloped them, redolent with the smells of baking bread and bubbling stew.

They'd all made it, praise God.

All, that was, except for Susan Haines and Mary Pillsbury, who'd gone off together just before the storm hit, Seeker explained.

Heck relayed this news, along with what Tom had done, to the others.

Instantly, men started talking of going out to find them, but Heck explained that would result only in death.

"But my dear, dear Mary!" a distraught Mrs. Pillsbury grieved.

"And my lovely Susan," a ghostly pale Titus Haines lamented.

"It's up to Tom now," Heck said. "He's a good man, and you're just going to have to trust him."

And then, as if summoned by Heck's faith in him, a snow-blind Tom Mullen stumbled through the door with two little girls, both badly frightened but very much alive.

CHAPTER 34

At last, winter broke. Temperatures still dipped below freezing some nights, but the April days were bright and sunny, warming into the upper 40s and low 50s.

Birds returned, twittering cheerfully, and game once more dotted the fields. A happy gurgling suffused the world as ice and snow melted.

When temperatures spiked briefly into the 60s and a heavy rain fell, the flash flood they'd been awaiting came roaring down the valley. It thumped and boomed and went on its way, dumping soil and trees and stones along the bottom land... but the levee held, protecting the new road.

For those who'd wintered in Heck's Valley, it was an exciting time.

Back East, folks were hitting the trail again. To some of those in Heck's Valley, the thought of this migration rekindled dreams of Oregon or California. For others, it spurred them to build homes and businesses before the emigrants passed this way.

First, however, they needed to prepare for something more pressing. They all knew the story of Seeker's parents and understood that sooner or later, Sioux raiders would ride into the valley.

"They will come here," Black Cloud said, while he and Heck sat their horses in a grassy valley to the south. "After the new grass turns this place green, they will come here. Then they will ride north to you."

"We will be ready for them," Heck said.

"I will also be ready. It is why I remain here, why my family spent the winter here instead of the mountains. I promised my ancestors and my nephew to punish the men who killed my sister."

Heck nodded at that. "It will be good to fight alongside you. How many enemies will come?"

"Between ten and twenty. They will be young and strong and hungry for glory."

"I'm fixing to send them to eternal glory."

"But this is not a war party. They will ride for plunder and to build their names. If we hit them hard, they will turn and run."

"And then will the war party come?"

Black Cloud sat staring out into the pale brown expanse of the valley, his face impassive. "Perhaps. This will depend on many things. Mostly the chief and his shamans. But also, how we handle the raiders. If we rout them, the Sioux may decide we are not worth the trouble. If we merely wound a few, they might be encouraged and send many warriors ready to kill or die."

"Well, I guess we'd better make sure and kill them all, then," Heck said.

Black Cloud nodded soberly. "All but one. He will carry the message back."

They sat for a while. Heck pictured the raiders coming upriver, pictured himself and the men of the compound firing from both sides of the valley.

"I will move here to this place," Black Cloud said. "I will make my camp on the slope, where I will see the raiders enter the valley. When I see them, I will build a fire of green boughs. When you see smoke, prepare to strike."

"What if they come at night?"

"They will not come at night. They are raiders, not warriors."

"What if they see your smoke?"

"I will wait for them to ride into the valley. They will not see the smoke. But you must see it because there will not be much time."

"We will keep a watcher at all times, Black Cloud. We will be ready."

CHAPTER 35

Heck's Valley once more sang with the music of saws and hammers and progress.

Before his untimely death, Jacob Fox had marked out lots for the town they might build. Most of these were upstream from Fort Seeker. Only the Pillsburys would build downstream, planting their farms on the opposite side of the river.

First came Burt Bickle's small cabin, barn, and corral, the whole of it fronted by the nice *Bickle Freighting* sign Myles Mason had carved over the winter.

Next came the cabin and business place Myles the furniture maker and undertaker would share with woodcutter and blooming entrepreneur Abe Zale and Will Ayers, who had decided to start his carpentry business here rather than in California, where he assumed many carpenters had already flocked.

Once these men finished their new homes and businesses, they helped build a place for the Widow and her son. Paul had grown over the winter and stood straighter. The changes he had experienced in the wake of combat had not departed. In fact, they had deepened, thanks not only to new confidence but also the influence of his new friend, Seeker, and the way the other children treated this pair of young men.

Meanwhile, the four men still determined to leave the valley —Trace Boon, Jem Pulcher, Mark Branch, and Amos Johnson readied their wagon, lingering to aid in the defense against the raiders. Amos had spent countless hours this winter sketching Heck and others and writing the story not only of Heck but also Heck's Valley.

Doc, whose arm had healed nicely, had decided to stay, as had Titus Haines, much to the pleasure of the Mullens. "I must stay," Titus explained one mild Sunday after services had concluded. "Otherwise, these children will descend into savagery."

"I'm so glad," Hope said. "I'm certain Tom would have left us otherwise."

Heck nodded. "Especially since Titus finally came to his senses about the courtship."

After Tom rescued Titus's younger daughter, Titus gave Tom permission to court Amelia. It was understood that the courtship would move slowly, but Tom and Amelia were no longer restricted to mere friendship.

Needless to say, they were very happy.

Hope had a pronounced bump now, and her face glowed with health. To Heck, she had never looked more beautiful. He loved to place his hand on her stomach and feel the baby kick. And when they were alone, he loved to crouch down and talk to his child, telling him or her how much he loved them.

Not that pregnancy had been all sighs and summer days.

Lately, Hope had been having trouble sleeping. She'd started limping as well, thanks to stiffness in her back and left leg and a line of fire that burned down that hamstring, behind the knee, and down the calf muscle before curling across the bottom of her foot.

Heck knew Hope was suffering some days, but she bore up under it, staying active, keeping a positive attitude, and never complaining... to him, at least. He figured she was probably sharing her woes more freely with her mother, Amelia, and Veronica Pillsbury, who would deliver the baby.

The Pillsbury men and Franky spent their days plowing bottom land across the river.

That's what they were doing on a beautiful afternoon when Franky came galloping across the river, hollering, "Smoke! Smoke to the south!"

CHAPTER 36

The cry spread throughout the community, which moved as one. Everyone knew what he or she had to do.

If the moments after Franky's alarm looked like they had been rehearsed, that's because they had been. Many times, in fact.

The horses and mules were driven back inside the fort. The pigs were already inside. There wasn't time to drive the other stock.

The women, each of them armed with a rifle, climbed into the towers, ready to defend the children inside.

The men hurried to their predetermined positions.

Most of the men crossed the river, rifles in hand. Reaching the other side, they walked backwards to the half-plowed field where they united with the Pillsburys and hid themselves on the slopes overlooking the other side of the valley just south of the compound.

On this side, Heck waited behind the levee along with

Seeker, Paul, and Abe Zale, who everyone said was a crack shot.

Each of them had an extra rifle ready to go, along with a pistol to use if the Indians withstood the double volley and charged.

Abe Zale grinned like a kid about to jump out and scare his brother.

Paul had lost his swagger. The boy looked pale and nervous, which pleased Heck. After all, Paul understood the danger they faced. Any show of confidence now would be either false bravado or foolhardiness, and either of those things could get the boy killed.

If Paul did what he was supposed to do and survived this encounter, he would grow again, Heck knew. It was the reason he'd asked the boy to join them in this position.

"Been waiting for this for a long time," Seeker said. He glared downstream, ready to kill.

Heck read uncharacteristic tension in his little brother's gritted teeth and white knuckles.

Usually, when it came to fighting, Seeker was a stone-cold killer. But today, rage had clearly shaken him.

Heck laid a hand on Seeker's back and smiled easily. "We're gonna do some good work today, little brother. This is no different from any other fight. These men are no different than any others we've faced."

Seeker's eyes flashed with emotion. "Yes, they are, Heck. They killed Ma and Pa."

"While they still live, they're just enemies, same as anybody else. When the shooting's over, you can consider the rest of it. Until then, though, I need you level-headed, not angry or excited."

Seeker exhaled heavily and nodded. "All right, Heck. I'll do like you say."

Five minutes later, fourteen Indians rode into view, scanning their surroundings and slowing to examine the half-plowed field and the backward tracks of the men now waiting uphill from and behind them.

Of course, to the Indians, those backward tracks made it look like the men had panicked and run back to the fort.

The raiders crossed the river, eyeing the fort upstream and angling toward the livestock.

Glancing to his right, Heck saw the others squinting down their rifles, ready to fire. "Easy," he reminded them in a whisper. "Wait for me to fire, then fire at will."

"Who's Will?" Paul whispered.

Heck chuckled softly. "Fire at will means once you shoot, you just keep reloading and shooting until it's over."

Paul nodded, getting it, and they all fell silent, which was good, because the Indians were now only two hundred yards away.

Keep coming, he thought, ready to fire if something spooked them. He wanted them inside one hundred yards but not much closer.

So he waited, the butt of the Hawken planted firmly in his shoulder. He stared down the barrel, which he and the others had covered in burlap to keep flashing sunlight from giving away their position.

His body was calm, cold, ready. His mind slowed everything, and the Indians rode forward with exquisite slowness, allowing him to study the men's appearance and action before choosing his target.

That one, he thought, identifying one slightly older man as the likely leader. He rode at the front of the pack, his face hard, his eyes wary. From his belt hung a profusion of dried scalps.

He was one of the men who killed Seeker's parents, Heck thought, and there was no dissenting voice in his head. *And he would happily chop through our gate and kill Hope and my child if I allowed it.*

Which I won't.

He pulled the trigger, the Hawken kicked him in the shoulder, and a bloom of black powder smoke clouded the air—but not before he saw the man jerk and topple from his horse, nailed through the heart.

As the guns beside him roared, Heck switched rifles and fired again.

The riders broke and turned back downstream.

Beside him, Heck's friends fired again.

The double volley had unseated five riders, and two more looked to be badly wounded.

With supreme calm, Heck reloaded his Hawken, shouldered it, and fired again, knocking another man from his saddle.

"Die!" Seeker shouted, having reloaded as quickly as Heck, and fired another round, cutting down another brave.

Beyond Seeker, Paul and Abe were still reloading.

Heck and Seeker rapidly reloaded in hopes of firing a fourth volley.

But the Indians streaked away, sprinting across the river, their horses' hooves pitching first plumes of sparkling water then divots of mud into the soil as they pounded away toward the south...

Directly into the trap Heck had devised for them.

"Come on, men!" Heck said, jumping to his feet and charging toward the river.

Seeker gave a bloodcurdling howl and sprinted alongside him, while Paul and Abe followed after, ready and willing.

A many-layered explosion rolled across the steep slope. Heck saw blooms of smoke where his friends had been lying in wait.

Seconds later, two Indians came streaking back in this direction. This time, they did not cross the river but stayed on the other side, heading north with their bodies laid low against their sprinting steeds.

Heck found his mark, swung his barrel, tracking the lead raider, and pulled the trigger.

His trusty Hawken boomed again, unseating the man.

Beside him, Seeker took his shot, and the final rider hit the ground.

Heck slung the rifle over his shoulder, drew his Colt, and jogged forward to check on the downed Indians.

The Sioux were crafty warriors not above playing possum, so he approached with care, but the men in the pasture were all stone-dead.

The goats and sheep had run off a bit. The cattle stood steady, stoically chewing their cuds.

The two men across the river looked very dead, lying in broken heaps upon the stones, but Heck figured he'd check them anyway.

Before he reached the river, however, someone cried out downstream.

CHAPTER 37

A small Indian came off the ground, swinging at one of the Pillsburys, a sliver of glinting steel jutting from his fist.

The farmer leapt back just in time, and Mr. Mullen surged forward and struck the back of the Indian's head with the butt of his rifle.

The Indian went down, and they swarmed him.

By the time Heck reached them, the raider had regained consciousness. He was just a kid, probably around Seeker's age, but he shouted and snarled, spewing violent threats in a tongue only Heck, Seeker, and Amos could understand.

It wasn't standard Sioux. The boy spoke some strange, offshoot dialect Heck had never heard before but still mostly understood.

The kid had been shot in the shoulder and was bleeding pretty heavily. One eye was swollen shut, probably from where he'd fallen off his horse, and of course, his head couldn't be doing too well after a blow with the butt of a Hawken.

This didn't stop the boy from insulting their manhood and threatening to kill all of them.

Heck respected the kid for that. He was a warrior through and through. He just hadn't gotten his size yet.

They had disarmed him and trussed him up like a calf, though, so even if he'd been seven feet tall, he couldn't have done much.

"Doc, get that bleeding stopped if you can," Heck said.

Doc nodded, crouched beside the boy, and began examining the gunshot wound, much to the consternation of the boy, who thrashed and shouted, trying to bite his physician.

"Why bother, Heck?" Jem Pulcher asked. "I don't speak Injun, but I still know what he wants to do to me. Why not just kill him?"

Heck shook his head. "We're sending him back. Let him tell his chief that we're nobody to fool with."

"I'm not sure that'll work, Heck," Will Ayers said. "I don't think he's afraid of us."

"No, he's not," Heck admitted. "And his chief won't be, either. You can't scare the Sioux. All you can do is make them understand they're better off leaving you alone. We hit them hard today. They'll feel this loss and think twice before coming after us... especially if we send an eyewitness back."

"Heck's right," Titus said. "It's a solid military tactic."

"Can you talk to him, Heck?" Mr. Mullen asked.

Heck nodded. "I'll talk to him, once he shuts up long enough for me to get a word in."

"Want me to gag the little wolf?" A.J. Plum asked.

"Nah, I'll get his attention," Heck said. Crouching down, he stared into the eyes of the boy for several seconds, keeping his expression neutral.

The boy, who referred to himself as *Little Bull*, promised to cut out Heck's heart and eat it.

Heck stared a moment longer, no expression on his face, then pointed to his chest and said, "Chief."

Heck's use of the Sioux language shocked the boy briefly into silence.

Heck pointed to Doc. "Shaman." Then he gestured to the other men. "Strong rifles."

"You cower like women behind your rifles," Little Bull declared. "I demand a duel with knives!"

"Heck would chop you up into tiny bits," Seeker said in Sioux.

"I fight you, half-breed!" Little Bull spat, glaring venomously at Seeker. "It is the way of my people. I demand a duel. You must fight me or release me out of cowardice."

Heck was interested. He'd never heard of this custom. "What tribe are you from?"

Little Bull's dark eyes flashed with pride. "I am Bone Canyon Sioux."

"That's east of here maybe fifty miles," Amos said in English. "They're a bunch of tough *hombres*. Dueling culture. Idea is, one warrior can always challenge another to a duel. Or, if he's in really rough shape, he can challenge a whole tribe."

"And fight them at once?" Mr. Mullen asked incredulously.

Amos shook his head. "From what I understand, the way it usually works out, the tribe selects a champion. If the challenger wins his duel, they either set him free or send in another champion, their choice. Eventually, he either dies or wins their respect and leaves the scene."

Heck thought about this as the kid started issuing his demands again along with a stream of insults and dark promises.

It seemed to Heck a good custom, one that would save lives over time... the type of custom he wanted among neighbors.

"Does the fight have to end in death?" Heck asked.

"Nah," Amos said. "A man can quit. But you know Injuns. They'd sooner die than surrender. Besides, you surrender, you're lower than dog dirt in their eyes. They'd just torture you to death."

"Yeah," Heck said, "but what if someone is incapacitated, and the winner shows mercy?"

"I'm not sure. The Sioux ain't exactly known for their mercy. But I reckon maybe that'd be the end of it as far as they were concerned."

"All right, Little Bull," Heck said in the boy's language. "I will honor your demand."

"Good," Seeker said. "It's gonna be fun killing him."

"No, I will face him."

"Aw, come on, Heck," Seeker said. "I want to fight him."

"I know you do, little brother," Heck said in English, and that was the truth. He could see that Seeker did want to kill another Indian from the tribe that had butchered his parents, just as Little Bull wanted to kill Seeker.

Truth be told, Heck didn't know which boy would triumph. This kid Little Bull, wounded though he was, looked pretty tough. That was part of the reason Heck would face him. The other reason, however, had to do with Heck's plans, both short term and long.

"I have spoken, Seeker," Heck said in Sioux. "I will fight Little Bull."

CHAPTER 38

Seeker issued no further challenges but simply stared daggers at the boy, who returned his hateful glare and said, "After I kill your chief, I will kill you, too, half-breed!"

"Little Bull makes threats like a child," Heck said. "In our tribe, threats are for the weak. We do not talk about deeds we will do. We do them!"

Saying this, he stripped away his gear, handing over his rifle and Colt and tomahawk to different folks, then pulled off his jacket and drew his Bowie.

"Why bother?" Jem Pulcher asked. "We got this kid right where we want him. I can just stomp his head to a pulp right now."

Heck shook his head, thinking he was glad Pulcher was moving on. The man lacked character. "I know what I'm doing, Jem. Set him loose and let him have his knife back."

The men looked at Heck with surprise, then formed a loose circle, giving the duelists plenty of space.

Jem let the kid loose and retreated, and someone tossed Little Bull's knife to the ground at his feet.

Little Bull grabbed the knife and stood with difficulty, almost managing to mask his considerable pain behind a peal of what was clearly intended as malicious laughter.

"If you defeat me, you are free to return to your people," Heck said.

"Then prepare to die, white man!" Little Bull said and rushed forward, swinging the knife with his left—and probably non-dominant—hand. His right arm swung like a dead weight thanks to the shoulder wound.

Heck respected the kid's spirit but wasn't about to underestimate him or take any unnecessary risks.

As Little Bull charged, Heck sidestepped and swept the boy's leg, tripping him.

Little Bull fell to the ground, struggled to his feet again, and whirled around, slashing the air with his blade.

Heck stepped forward.

Little Bull, without the slightest glint of fear in his eyes, limped forward, whipping the blade back and forth.

Heck timed the attacks and lashed out with his boot, kicking the boy square in the chest and knocking him from his feet.

The kid fell onto his back with a grunt, lost his knife, and started to reach for it, but Heck slammed his boot into the kid's temple and knocked him out cold.

There was no joy in bludgeoning a child into unconsciousness, but he knew he'd made the right move.

When the boy awoke, they lifted him atop his horse.

Little Bull looked absolutely dejected. "You did not kill me."

"No. I could have, but I showed mercy."

"You will regret it. Someday, I will come back here and kill you. And I will kill the half-breed and all these others."

"I find your threats womanly," Heck said, knowing he had a role to play and that it needed to be played perfectly if they were to avoid war. "If you are going to kill me, kill me, but do not waste air talking of it."

Little Bull merely stared, his dark eyes boiling with rage.

"Tell your chief that this valley belongs to Killing Oak."

The boy's eyes changed at the mention of the name the Rocky Mountain Utes had given Heck. It was a subtle change, well concealed, but there nonetheless, and Heck knew the boy had heard of him.

Good.

"Tell your chief Killing Oak would live in peace. Killing Oak does not want the land of the Bone Canyon Sioux. But if the Bone Canyon Sioux come here looking for death, they will find it. Killing Oak will kill anyone who means his people harm."

And with that, they sent the boy downstream with his own horse and plenty of food and water but no knife or bow or rifle.

"Something tells me we haven't seen the last of that kid," Doc said.

"Yeah, something tells me the same thing," Heck said.

"Good," Seeker said. "I hope he comes back. I want to kill him, too."

Heck put an arm around the boy's shoulders. "You might just get the chance, little brother. You two are of an age. Sooner or later, you might just get a chance."

Everyone packed up and headed for the fort, but Heck headed downstream to thank Black Cloud for his help.

"Come with me, Seeker," he said.

Seeker fell in beside him, and together, they walked along the river, heading for the switchback trail.

"Well, how does it feel, little brother?" Heck asked once they'd walked a way.

"How does what feel?"

"Avenging your parents."

"Oh. Good, I guess. I'm glad they're dead."

"But…"

Seeker shrugged. "I don't know. I thought it would feel better was all. I dreamed of this since… you know."

"Well, you did what you had to do. So you should feel good."

"Like I said, I'm glad we killed them. But I guess I pictured it being more personal. Like them knowing who I was and why I was killing them. Do you think they were the ones that killed Ma and Pa?"

"Some of them, anyway."

Seeker nodded. "I guess that's why I wanted to fight that kid so bad. I see now why you did what you did, but I wanted to kill him face-to-face. I wanted him to know why I was killing him."

"Well, like I said, you still might get the chance. When we get home, I'm gonna teach you how to fight with knives."

CHAPTER 39

The following day, the four bachelors left for the trail and whatever fortunes—and women—they might find on the west coast.

They had only one wagon and a single team of oxen, but Heck and the others made sure they were well provisioned for the trip.

"You'll be the first of the season to reach California," Heck said, shaking Amos's hand. "Good luck, my friend."

"Thanks, Heck. I'll miss you. And you, too, Hope. Thank you both for saving me after the bear attack, and I sure do appreciate you killing that big old grizzly, Heck."

"My pleasure," Heck said. "Especially considering he was fixing to eat me if I didn't."

Everyone was gathered around, wishing the men well, so it took a while. Finally, Heck caught up to Trace Boon.

"Thanks for saving us, Heck," Trace said, holding out his hand, "and thanks for letting us winter here."

Heck shook his hand. "Good luck out there. And Trace, remember, not a word about the gold. Right?"

"Not a word," Trace said.

"They couldn't get it out of us with torture, Heck," Jem Pulcher said, sticking out his hand.

Heck shook it, said goodbye to Mark Branch, and then watched as the men marched off, followed by the cheering of the citizens of Heck's Valley.

It struck Heck then that that's what they were now. Citizens.

He said as much to Doc, who stood nearby.

"What do you mean?" Doc asked.

"Well, everyone who'd planned to leave just left," Heck explained. "So I guess that makes the rest of us citizens."

"I guess you're right," Doc said with a smile. He panned his bespectacled gaze over the lots and new structures beyond the palisade. "We're becoming a town."

"Which means we'll be needing a name for little hamlet," Mr. Mullen said with a mischievous smile.

Hope grinned at him. "What are you up to, Daddy? And why are you smiling like that, Doc? In fact, why is everyone smiling?"

Heck looked around, noticing their faces with the same confusion Hope had expressed. He had the distinct impression that the whole citizenry of this unnamed little town was having some premeditated fun with his wife and him.

"All right," he said. "What's the big joke?"

"Oh, it's no joke, my boy," Mr. Mullen said, clapping him on the shoulder. "We're dead serious."

"About what?"

"About the name of our town," Doc said. "We met and discussed it. Voted on it, even."

"You voted on a town name?" Heck said. "Nobody told us."

"You don't get to control everything, big brother," Seeker laughed. "We figured it out without you."

"Hold on," Heck said. "You knew, too? And you didn't tell me?"

Seeker threw back his head with a squawk of wild laughter.

"All right," Hope said, grinning through her confusion. "Go ahead, tell us what name you've decided on for the town."

"Amelia suggested it," Mr. Mullen said, putting his hands on his daughter's shoulders and smiling at her, his eyes shining with love. "And we all thought it was a wonderful idea and approved the name by unanimous vote. My dear, welcome to Hope City."

CHAPTER 40

Over the next few weeks, school was canceled, and everyone worked like oxen from dawn to dusk, plowing, planting, cutting and dragging timber, and building houses.

Hope City was coming to life.

Hope was both flattered and embarrassed by the name, arguing that she didn't deserve such a distinction, but Heck agreed with the others wholeheartedly, and the town was officially dubbed as Hope City by a final vote of 32-1, with only Hope voicing opposition.

Doc, Ray, and Sam built a large cabin with an office where Doc could see patients. Everyone else pitched in to build a new schoolhouse, knowing that emigrants would soon be arriving at Badger's Trading Post. Behind the school, they laid the foundation for the cabin Titus would share with his daughters.

Next door would be A.J. Plum's cabin with plenty of room for the whole Plum family, which would soon grow larger since

Mrs. Plum was pregnant again. For the time being, A.J. Plum continued to run his blacksmith shop out of the fort. Only a fool moves an anvil, let alone a forge, unnecessarily.

Sam Collins wasn't sure about his long-term plans, which hinged completely on gold. If more gold was found and prospectors moved into the region, he would set up the first assayer's shop in the territory. For now, he would continue his life as a general laborer until Heck was ready to transport the big nugget to San Francisco.

Downstream, the Pillsburys split their time between plowing, planting, and starting their cabins. Happily, like Hope and Mrs. Plum, both Pillsbury women were pregnant again.

They worked with their rifles at hand, knowing at any time the Bone Canyon Sioux could descend upon them in great number, though Heck hoped the chief had received his message and embraced its logic.

Then one day, while Heck was helping push a log up a ramp onto the wall of what would become the Haines's cabin, Doc called out, "Indians coming!"

Instantly, the men dropped their tools and picked up their rifles, but as Heck looked up and saw the riders and the wagon coming around the bend behind them, he leaned his rifle back against the wall and announced, "It's okay, men. Put down your rifles. These are friends."

He smiled incredulously, then strode forward and met the first rider, who reined in his horse and lifted a hand.

Heck raised his own hand. "Welcome to the valley, Two Bits."

Then, as the Shoshone woman's horse, a beautiful buckskin

with a mane as glossy and black as the hair of its rider, reached them, Heck nodded and matched her warm smile. "Good afternoon, Mrs. Bridger."

A moment later, the wagon arrived, and a smiling Jim Bridger hopped down.

Heck held out his hand. Jim took it then hauled him into an embrace, pounding Heck on the back.

"Hello, Heck. Still in one piece?"

"More or less. You?"

Jim nodded. "It's good to see you, my young friend. And good to see what you're doing here. I saw the sign. Heck's Valley, Hope City, Fort Seeker. What are you doing, building a town?"

Heck nodded. "That's right. A lot's changed since I last visited."

"I can see that, my friend."

"Well, come on in. We'll take care of your animals and get you folks a nice meal."

"Sounds good," Jim said. "And I brought a wagon load of supplies to trade or sell if you're game."

"Oh, I'm game all right."

"Figured you might be. Wait till you see the chickens."

"Chickens?" Heck said with excitement.

"Prime laying chickens. It was a chore, keeping them warm over this miserable winter." Jim grinned with amusement. "But when you hear what I'm gonna charge you for them, you'll see it was well worth my trouble."

Heck laughed. "Supply and demand."

"That's right. You stay on the right side of supply and demand, you'll always be fat and happy."

"You've been telling me that since I was fourteen."

"So I have, so I have." Jim's smile faltered, and he lowered his voice. Others were arriving on foot now. "Later, when we're alone, I have news for you."

Heck felt a stab of concern. He could tell by Jim's tone that it wasn't good news. But now was not the time to ask for more details, so Heck just nodded and said, "All right."

Jim slapped him on the back. "It sure is good to see you, Heck. You look bigger and stronger than ever. Have any trouble since I saw you?"

"A bit," Heck said, figuring he'd share the stories of Dave Chapman, the bears, and the Indian skirmishes for later. Now, as Hope stepped up to his side, he said, "Jim, I'd like you to meet my wife, Hope. Hope, this is Mr. Jim Bridger."

Beaming, Hope gave a little curtsey, which she executed gracefully despite her current condition. "Mr. Bridger, it is a pleasure. I've heard so much about you."

That night, they had a joyous feast. Everyone had heard of their guest, of course, since Jim Bridger was one of the most famous frontiersmen in the nation, but even if he hadn't been famous, they would have treated him like a king for bringing the load of supplies... especially the crates of chickens.

The women in particular were excited, understanding that from this point forward, their kitchens would benefit tremendously from the availability of eggs. And since there were roosters in the mix, Heck's Valley would soon have no shortage of chickens or eggs.

Mary Bridger hit it off with Hope and Amelia, and while they chatted, Heck and Jim went outside to talk in private.

As Heck left the cabin, he looked forward to talking with his old friend.

Of course, at that point, Heck had no idea that their conversation would change his life forever.

CHAPTER 41

"This is a lovely place you're building, Heck," Jim said, "and these folks seem like the right kind to start a town."

Heck nodded. "They're good people."

"Most people are, you get to know them," Jim said. Then his attitude shifted. "Do any of them have money?"

Heck shrugged. "No idea. Why?"

"Well, I'm just wondering, since they seem to like this place, if they might want to invest in your venture."

"What is it, Jim? What's the news?"

"There's a problem with the land."

Heck braced himself. "What sort of problem?"

"The General Land Office—that's who I went through for my ground—has been absorbed by the Department of the Interior."

"What's that mean?"

"Basically? It means more money."

"How much?"

"Able Dean—that's my lawyer; good man, Able—he talked to them, and they said you can have the ground. That's the good news right there. Half the battle is getting them to agree to it, you know? But they want four dollars an acre now."

Heck grunted. "So… fifteen thousand, two hundred for the ground I want. Lot of money."

"Sure is. And that's just for the land, you understand. After agency costs and lawyer fees, you'll need at least fifteen thousand, five hundred."

"That's more than I have."

Jim nodded. "I was afraid you were going to say that. Sorry to be the bearer of bad tidings, Heck. How short are you? I could lend you a thousand or two."

"Thanks, Jim, but my pa told me to never go into debt."

"Wise man, your pa. But this ground, it might be worth it."

"Oh, it's worth it, all right. I just don't have the money and don't want to go into debt."

"I can have Able write it up for less acreage and resubmit if you want. He's got everything ready to roll. He just needs to get your go-ahead and hand the money to the receiver, and they'll lock this ground up and get to work on the title."

Heck thought it through. He had gotten used to the notion of owning this land—all 3800 acres of it. Owning less would be a disappointment.

He weighed his options. "What if I wanted more?"

Jim laughed. "That isn't normally how it works, my young friend. More land costs more money, not less."

"I know, Jim, but what if I came into some money?"

"You fixing to pan for gold? I hate to discourage an ambitious man, but that's hard work, and almost nobody makes out.

By the time you find anything, somebody might catch wind of it and grab the land right from under you."

"I already found some."

Jim grinned. "You already found gold?"

Heck nodded.

"Enough to make a difference?"

"Enough to make a big difference," Heck confessed. "Come on inside, and I'll show you."

He led Jim into the cave cabin and barred the door and lit a lantern and took him back into the storage room, which smelled like heaven, thanks to all the apples still piled there. He uncovered the stones in front of Seeker's hidey hole then pulled out the nugget.

"Well, I'll be," Jim laughed. "That's the biggest nugget I've seen... by about ten times. Heck, you lead a charmed life."

"I don't know about charmed—wait till you hear about the troubles we had this winter—but I praise God for this blessing, anyway."

"I should say so. What's it weigh?"

"A hundred pounds."

Jim whistled with astonishment. "A hundred pounds?"

"At least."

"Pure gold?"

"That guy you met, Sam Collins, he's an assayer. He thinks it's pure gold all the way through."

"What's he think you can get per ounce? It's gotta be higher than the going rate for dust."

"That's what he said. Last he knew, dust was selling for sixteen dollars an ounce. Sam thinks if we sell to the right buyer, a wealthy collector might pay twenty dollars an ounce. Maybe more."

"I wouldn't be surprised. I really wouldn't. This is quite an oddity. So you're probably looking at somewhere between twenty-five thousand and thirty-two thousand dollars."

"That's what I figure. Thing is, if I'm gonna sell this to pay for ground, I'd want to buy even more land. Could Mr. Dean make that happen?"

"Oh yeah, like I said, Able's a good man. He knows folks over there in the Department of the Interior, too. He could get you a big chunk of ground. What are you thinking?"

"Maybe double the size to 7600 acres."

"That'd be almost twelve square miles."

"Yup. I'd like to tack on another mile to the West and another mile to the south. That way, I'd own a lot of grass south of here and a good stretch to the west. A friend and his family are living a couple of valleys over. They're talking of leaving, but if they change their minds, at least they'd always have a place to stay."

"That the Shoshone you mentioned? Black Cloud?"

"Right."

"Mary's heard of him. Says he's a great warrior."

"That has yet to be seen, but he does carry himself with confidence, and he gave me some help with a bunch of Sioux raiders not long ago."

"Sounds like a good man to leave a stake for. But hold on a second. I gotta ask: have you thought about how, exactly, you would sell a nugget this big?"

"Sam says to go through a lawyer. He says to hunt for

specialty buyers, collectors, and get them to bid against each other."

"Good advice. I'm sure Able could find buyers and set up an auction. Trouble is, he's all the way in San Francisco. Which is probably the only spot west of the Mississippi where you're going to find folks willing to shell out the kind of money you're hunting."

"That's what I was thinking. But how would I get it there safely?"

Jim shrugged. "Well, you'd need some good men to ride with you. And I guess you'd have to make it look like something nobody would want to steal."

"Nobody knows this country like you, Jim. Would you help me get it there?"

"You know I will. I've been dying of cabin fever over at the fort anyway. Question is, how do we disguise it? What do we make it look like? What would no one try to steal?"

It took only a second for Heck to come up with the answer. He grinned. "I think I got that covered."

CHAPTER 42

"Sure, I can make you a coffin," Myles said. "It'll be a bear, sawing the planks, but I can get on it tomorrow, if you want. Who died?"

Heck told him what he had in mind.

Myles laughed. "That's good. We can pack hay in there real tight. That way, it won't roll around."

"Good idea," Heck said. "Make it strong, Myles."

———

LATER THAT NIGHT, HECK AND HOPE RETURNED TO THEIR CABIN, and he told her the news.

He hated to leave her, especially with the baby coming, but he couldn't risk losing the valley.

He loved this place. Hope loved it, too. And with Hope City coming together, a lot of people were counting on living here.

As he explained these things, Hope stayed strong.

He knew that if he had given her the same news a few months earlier, she would have sobbed uncontrollably, but as her pregnancy had progressed, she had regained control of her emotions. If anything, she seemed stronger than ever.

"How long would you be gone?" Hope asked.

"It's a thousand miles each way. It'll take me three or four months. Maybe longer, depending on how long things take in San Francisco."

Her lips parted slightly. "That means…"

He nodded. "I won't be here when the baby comes. I'm sorry, Hope."

Hope nodded. He could see she was struggling, but she said, "Mother will be with me. And Veronica. And you'll be back… in August."

"I'm sorry it has to be this way, Hope, but I'll get home as quick as I can, and once I take care of all this, it really will be home. It'll be ours."

Hope nodded again. "Thank you for doing this, Heck. Thank you for going to such great lengths to make this our home and to provide everything our babies will ever need."

Heck knew she was being brave, knew she was conflicted, knew she was being strong for him. But he also believed she was being strong for herself—and needed him to be strong for her.

"Thank you for being so brave, Hope. If you weren't so strong, I could never do this."

She smiled. "I come from fighting stock."

He laughed. "I know you do. I thank God for you every day, and I can't wait to meet our son or daughter."

"Son."

"We'll see."

"I've told you all along, Mr. Martin. I am carrying your son."

"Well, I'll hurry home either way. And if it is a boy, I expect we're gonna have quite a scrapper on our hands."

CHAPTER 43

J une 1851

ON A SWELTERING AFTERNOON FORTY-FOUR DAYS AFTER LEAVING
Hope City, they finally reached San Francisco. They had
completed the trip with amazing speed thanks to Jim Bridger's
tremendous knowledge of the land and the toughness and
single-mindedness of the men.

Unused to such rigorous travel, Sam Collins limped into the
city.

As they walked the streets, Two Bits unfastened the sling in
which he'd been supporting his arm. The bullet wound from
their skirmish with a band of Utes was healing well.

Even at forty-seven years of age, Jim Bridger remained tire-
less, and Heck felt great.

For as much as he missed Hope—and he missed her terribly —and for as distracting as it was, wondering about his child, the time on the trail had done him good. He loved to travel, loved pushing his body, eating beside a campfire, and sleeping under the stars.

That being said, he was ready for a bath and a good meal.

Seeing the sprawling bayside city for the first time, Heck felt amazed, repulsed, and curious.

"Forty thousand people," Heck said with a shake of his head. "How do they all fit?"

"I'm betting most of them are asking the same question," Jim said. "It's going to be a trick to find anyplace to stay here, and from what I've heard, room rates are beyond ridiculous. You can always come out and join us at camp."

A few miles outside of town, Jim had already scouted out the spot where he and Two Bits would be staying.

"We'll ask around about a room," Heck said, "but I wouldn't be surprised if we're back in camp tonight."

"I'm looking forward to a bath and a good meal," Sam Collins said. The young assayer had held up well on the trail despite its rigors and thereby gained new respect among the other men.

"Sounds good," Heck said, "but before we do anything else, I reckon we'd best do something with the nugget. Some of these folks look pretty rough."

San Francisco was unlike anything Heck had ever seen before. There were people everywhere, most of them rough-looking men he assumed were either miners or ruffians.

The city clearly wasn't ready for its population explosion. In 1848, the population had been only 1000.

Now, there were people everywhere, vast tent towns, and a harbor absolutely jammed with ships. Boats were everywhere. Some, run aground, served as saloons, hotels, bordellos, gambling halls, dry goods stores, or assayers' offices.

Making matters worse, just a month ago, eighteen blocks— over two thousand buildings, including the business district— had burned in a great fire... only three days after a major earthquake.

And yet, folks persisted. The vast, blackened heart of town already rang with hammers.

"Good idea," Jim Bridger said. "Some of these fellas look like they'd steal a casket for the change of clothes inside. I'd hate to bring it all this way just to get robbed. But where in the world will you hide it?"

Heck grinned. "I know just the place."

———

"MIGHTY NICE CROSS YOU GENTLEMEN MADE," THE GRAVEYARD keeper said, indicating the crude marker at the head of the grave in which laid the coffin they'd brought from Heck's Valley.

"We wanted to do right by him," Heck said. "Old Biscoe didn't have two pennies to rub together, but he still deserves a decent burial."

The graveyard keeper nodded somberly. "Would any of you like to say a few words about your friend?"

Heck and his friends stood around the grave with their hats in their hands.

"Aaron was a good fellow," Jim Bridger said.

Heck nodded solemnly. "Yeah, he was rock solid."

"You could even say he had a heart of gold," Sam said.

None of them dared say more for fear of laughing, which would have been highly inappropriate, given the situation.

"Well, that's a very nice sentiment, gentlemen. Friends like you are a blessing."

Leaving the graveyard, Sam suggested they celebrate with a drink, but neither Heck nor Jim drank.

"I will drink," Two Bits said with a wolfish grin.

"Oh no, you won't," Jim said. "Not while you're in my employ. You know what alcohol does to you."

The rugged Shoshone shrugged his thick shoulders and grumbled, "Just one drink."

"You take one drink, you'll be jailed for murder by midnight."

Two Bits continued to grumble but objected no further.

With that settled, they decided to have a celebratory meal instead.

They walked down to the waterfront.

"Watch yourselves here, gentlemen. There are pickpockets and muggers everywhere on the waterfront. And stay together. Otherwise, somebody will Shanghai you."

"What's that mean?" Heck asked.

"Means they hit you from behind, a whole gang of them, and beat you into unconsciousness. Then you wake up on a boat."

"Why?" Sam asked.

"While you're unconscious, you join a sailing crew," Jim said. "They have your signature and everything."

"The muggers forge it?" Heck asked.

"That's right," Jim said. "Press gangs prowl the dockside every night, looking for blood money."

Heck shook his head. He liked to think the best of people, but some folks did their best to ruin your faith in humanity.

They found a café serving seafood and fresh-baked bread. The prices were ridiculously high—a whole dollar for a slice of bread and two dollars if you wanted it buttered—but Heck told everyone to load up, his treat.

He appreciated these men, and after weeks of jerky and trail food, it was glorious, a proper celebration for reaching their destination.

And with over fourteen thousand dollars in Liberty Head double eagles, he could afford the tab. He carried three thousand dollars—around ten pounds of gold—in a leather money belt around his middle. The rest was stored in a steel lockbox built secretly into the wagon.

After the meal, Jim led them away from the waterfront to the tiny office of Able Dean.

Opening the door, Heck felt a thrill. So much hinged on what would happen in the next few moments.

CHAPTER 44

A smiling young man in an expensive suit stood up behind his desk. "Hello, Mr. Bridger."

Heck was surprised. From everything Jim had said, Able Dean was a top lawyer. This guy didn't look much older than Heck.

"Howdy, Terrance," Jim said, lifting a hand.

"I'll go fetch Mr. Dean for you."

"Thanks."

Terrance hurried off through the back of the office.

"His suit tricked me," Heck said.

"How's that?"

"I thought he was Dean."

Jim grinned. "That's his clerk."

"Dean must pay him well if he wears suits like that," Sam said.

Jim shrugged. "Maybe he pans for gold on the weekends."

A short while later, a lean, thirtyish man with a long,

straight nose, a dark goatee, and long hair swept back from a receding hairline came through the door.

He offered a pleasant smile. "Gentlemen."

He shook hands with Jim, nodded to Two Bits, then turned to Heck and held out his hand. "You must be Mr. Martin."

"Yes, sir," Heck said, shaking the man's hand.

"I'm Able Dean."

"That's what I figured, sir. Nice to meet you. And this is my friend, Sam Collins."

The two men shook hands and shared pleasantries.

Then Heck told the lawyer, "Thank you for working on the land for me."

"You're quite welcome, Mr. Martin. Happy to help. I'm assuming Jim delivered the bad news about the price per acre."

"Yes, sir, he did. But I think everything will work out."

Able Dean smiled. "I'm glad to hear that. Why don't you come and sit down, and we can talk everything through."

"Sounds good, sir."

"Now, how many chairs will we need? Will all of you men be staying while we discuss Mr. Martin's business?"

Though the question was ostensibly aimed at the others, Able Dean addressed the question to Heck, clearly giving him the opportunity to declare which men he wanted to stay.

Heck turned to the others, whom he trusted implicitly. "You sticking around, Jim?"

"Not unless you need me. Two Bits and I have some business in town. I have a few suppliers to see... if I'm lucky enough to find them after the fire."

"That was a terrible business," Mr. Dean said, shaking his

head. "Ten hours, that's all it took. Burned the city to the ground."

"That's what we heard on the trail coming here," Jim said. "Must have looked like Hades was swallowing up the whole affair."

"A lot of folks thought that's just what it was, God's judgement on this abomination. But most people just wanted someone to blame. Now, they're restless and demanding justice. Around a hundred just formed what they're calling the Committee of Vigilance to clean up crime around here. A week or two ago, they hung a man."

"Well, I'm glad you're all right, Able," Jim said.

The lawyer nodded. "Ever since moving here, I wished I had an office in the heart of the business district. What a blessing that I didn't."

Jim and Two Bits said their goodbyes and left.

"You want to stick around, Sam?" Heck asked.

"Sure thing, Heck."

"Outstanding," Able Dean said. "Terrance, an extra chair, please."

"Yes, sir," Terrance said, carrying over a chair that had been sitting in front of his desk. Heck would have offered to help, but it was a short trip, the desks being as close to one another.

"Well, let's review everything so far," Able Dean said.

Heck nodded.

The lawyer launched into his review, explaining everything Jim had already told Heck and showing him the paperwork waiting for the exact acreage, purchase price, and Heck's signature.

"The receiver is currently in town, so if you want to take

care of this immediately, we can probably wrap everything up tomorrow."

"Sounds good to me, sir," Heck said. "Though I have some business to tend to first."

"All right. Well, let me know when you have everything tied up. I'm assuming you don't have things surveyed yet."

"Not much," Heck said, leaving out the fact that the surveyor had been killed in a fight with Crow warriors.

"That's all right. With these big frontier purchases, we submit as many landmarks as we can and rough things out as well as possible. Then, when the Army comes through and surveys, you'll send me the information, and I'll have your deed updated. The important thing is getting the title before someone else. That might not seem likely now, but if someone finds a flake of gold in that country, folks will flock there."

Sam chuckled.

Able Dean raised one eyebrow and offered a slight grin. "You already found some color?"

"Yes, sir," Heck said. "We might need your help with that, too."

"I'm always happy to help you with anything, Mr. Martin, but you'll be better served by talking to an assayer about that."

Heck hooked a thumb toward his friend. "Sam's an assayer."

Able Dean looked perplexed. "Ah, so why...?"

"Heck found more than a spot of color," Sam explained. "In fact, I'd say his was a singular discovery. One that we'll probably want to sell by auction to a limited number of buyers of significant means and interest in such things."

"Well, I must say you men have piqued my interest. What, precisely, did you find, Mr. Martin?"

"A big old nugget," Heck said.

"How big?"

"A hundred pounds."

Able Dean's eyes bulged. "A hundred pounds." He turned to Sam. "What do your tests show? How rich is the ore?"

Sam smiled, clearly enjoying the moment. "You misunderstand, Mr. Dean. The nugget is pure gold."

"A hundred pounds of pure gold?" Able Dean said, his voice filled with awe.

Behind them, Terrance dropped a stack of papers.

"Sorry, sir," the young man said.

"Not a problem, Terrance. Go ahead and flip our sign to *Closed* and lock the door, please. We have serious business to attend to."

CHAPTER 45

Heck and Sam were in good spirits as they walked back through the waterfront. Remembering Jim Bridger's warnings, however, Heck remained alert.

"That went well," Sam declared.

"It sure did," Heck said. "Thanks for your help, Sam."

"My pleasure. I wonder how much you'll get for it?"

"Hard to say. Mr. Dean seemed optimistic, though."

"Yeah, and I'm glad he thought of several potential buyers right off the top of his head. That bodes well."

"In the meantime, my friend, I reckon we ought to get cleaned up. This restaurant Mr. Dean wants us to meet him at later sounds awful fancy."

"It does. What's it called again? Those Mexican words never stick in my head."

"*El Caballero*. Means horseman. But more than that, it means gentleman."

"Well, whatever it means, Mr. Dean sure did make the food

sound good. I guess you're right, though. We ought to get cleaned up." Sam looked down at his clothes and frowned. "Trouble is, after the trip, my other change of clothes is just as ragged and filthy as the ones I'm wearing."

Heck laughed. "Don't worry. We'll get you some new duds. I'll buy you whatever clothes you want. You can even get a suit like Terrance."

"Thanks, Heck," Sam said. "That would be real nice, though I sure don't need anything that fancy."

"Unfortunately, I won't be able to buy anything that fits. Being so tall, I gotta have everything special made, and that takes time."

"I hear these Chinamen are great tailors, though," Sam said. "You might be surprised."

"What do I need a suit for? I brought along a change of clothes. They're nothing fancy, but they'll do the job. Then we can get these duds laundered and maybe get ourselves laundered, too."

Sam laughed, and they continued along the teeming streets of the waterfront. Folks stared at Heck, probably because of his great height, he thought.

They went into a laundry and asked for a place to change and dropped their clothes at the counter and asked the Chinaman where they could find a good bath. He directed them to cut through the alley to one of the floating ship stores, a place called, not very creatively, The Bath House.

Taking the local economy into consideration, Heck tipped the man a whole dollar and went out.

Entering the dim alley, Heck felt his hackles rise.

This felt like a good place to get ambushed... or that thing Jim talked about, Shanghaied.

Heck drew his Colt and laid it against his thigh.

"What is it?" Sam asked, his voice frightened.

"Nothing. Just a good place for somebody to lay in wait. Empty alley, narrow walls, all these doors and windows."

Sam nodded and pulled his derringer.

A short time later, they reached the end of the alley without incident and came to the edge of the harbor, where a walkway led to a ship that had been converted into businesses. Haphazard scaffolding girdled the front of the boat, creating a walkway that wrapped around both sides.

From the prow of the boat hung two simple signs. The upper sign pointed to the right and read *Rooms*. The lower sign pointed left and read *Bath House*.

They holstered their weapons and went left. The walkway creaked under their footsteps, which clocked hollowly against the warped planks.

Going through the door, they took off their hats and were greeted by a smiling Chinese woman who spoke broken English but nonetheless managed to direct them down the hall, where she separated them, one man to a room.

"Don't forget to scrub behind your ears," Sam joked.

"Yeah, you make sure and get between your toes," Heck said, and went into his room.

It was a small space dominated by the biggest tub he'd ever seen. It was already full of water and looked surprisingly clean.

Beside the tub sat a chair. Above it, a line of pegs jutted from the wall. One held a towel. Another, a scrub brush. The others, he reckoned, were for him to hang up his clothes.

He did just that, stripping naked, and crawled into the luke-warm water. He took a washcloth and bar of soap from the edge of the tub and set to washing his face.

It felt good.

He figured it would take a bit to get his beard and hair clean.

The door opened.

Heck jerked his head upward and wiped water from his eyes and grabbed for his Colt, which he'd sat on the chair beside the bath.

A robed woman entered the room, saw the gun, and gave a frightened yelp.

Heck stared at her for a moment, his beard dripping water. Seeing no weapons, he set the pistol on the chair.

"Sorry," he said, feeling embarrassed for having frightened the woman who clearly worked here. "I didn't mean to scare you. I don't need anything, though. Everything's real nice."

Having recovered, the woman smiled, and opened her robe.

"Whoa!" Heck quickly averted his eyes from her nakedness. "Ma'am, what are you doing?"

"I bathe you," the woman said, her voice full of humor.

"No, ma'am. I'll bathe myself, thank you."

"You do not like me?" she asked. "You want other girl?"

"No, no girls. Not you, not anybody else. I'm a married man. I will wash myself."

"But sir, I make you feel good."

"Get out of here," Heck said, losing his patience. "I mean it. Get."

"Yes, sir."

He waited until he heard the door again and opened his eyes and saw that she had, indeed, left the room.

What kind of place was this?

He shook his head and set to scrubbing himself as quickly as he could. Then, he got out of the tub and toweled off and got back into his clothes and hurried out of the room, almost colliding with Sam, who charged into the hall at the same time, wearing a misbuttoned shirt and a rattled expression.

"Some girl visit you, too?" Heck asked.

Sam nodded. "Scared me half to death. Let's get out of this place."

"The faster the better," Heck said. "And the same goes for getting out of San Francisco. I see why folks thought God sent the earthquake and fire. This town is a den of iniquity."

CHAPTER 46

The door of Getty's Haberdashery swung open with a cheerful jingle, and four primitive men marched in, carrying a fifth man between them.

Bill Getty, who was both the proprietor of the shop and the most feared crime boss in the city, stepped away from the rack of ties he'd been examining and braced the men with a murderous look. "What in the name of tarnation do you men think you're doing, bringing that through my front door?"

Leo, always reliable, came off his stool to one side of the door and put his double-barreled coach gun on the intruders.

The men, whose rough faces already looked deathly pale, paled further. They backed up until they were supporting the unconscious man just outside the doorway.

"It's Danny, Mr. Getty," one of them said. "He got himself plugged while we was working the waterfront."

"Well, what excuse is that for getting blood on my floor?"

"I'm sorry, sir," a dark-haired man in a black derby hat said, "but it's Danny, sir. We was about to Shanghai this fella, and he plugged Danny through the guts."

"Then he's a dead man," Getty said. "Serves him right for getting shot. Take him behind the shop and hide him. Tonight, you can throw him in the water. But make sure and weigh him down first."

The man in the derby hat looked shocked. "But sir... it's Danny."

The wounded man moaned as if to emphasize the point.

Getty shut his eyes for a second, summoning patience. He knew Danny was well liked among the crew but had never understood why. He supposed it was the lad's quick smile and Irish lilt and the way he always joked around with the others.

But not with Getty, of course. No one joked with Getty.

He opened his eyes again. "All right. All right. Take him back to the flophouse, and I'll see about getting him a doctor. Krugler, you stay here."

A stocky, balding man with a dead eye and a truculent jaw stepped forward. "Yes, sir."

"Krugler, you're going to clean up this blood and go fetch the doctor while these other men transport poor Danny to his room."

"Yes, sir," Krugler said and waited without so much as a *fare thee well* while the others carried Danny away.

Unlike the others, Krugler didn't appear troubled by Danny's condition.

Which, of course, was no surprise to Getty.

Krugler had no soul.

That's why Getty kept him around.

"You have a mop, sir?" Krugler said.

"Leo will get it for you. Go ahead, Leo. Now, Mr. Krugler, forget about the doctor. I want you to take care of Danny yourself. Tell the other men the doctor will come, then get them out of the room and use a pillow on him. Do you understand?"

Krugler nodded, showing neither surprise nor hesitation. He was a filthy ape of a man who blanched at nothing. Which made him a very valuable employee indeed.

Krugler was mopping up the blood when the door opened again, the bell tinkled merrily, and the twit from down the street pranced in wearing one of the suits Getty had given him in a payment.

"Oh," the young man said, sidestepping the blood with a look of terror. "Oh my."

"What is it, Terrance?" Getty demanded. Something made him want to strangle the fop, but as always, Getty restrained himself.

After all, Terrance was every bit as valuable as Krugler in his way. He was one of the many informants Getty had in various offices of note throughout the city.

Skittering past the blood, Terrance gave a little bow. "Mr. Getty, sir. I have news." His eyes shone with boyish excitement that only increased Getty's desire to grab his skinny neck and choke the life from him.

"What is it, then? Don't just stand there grinning at me. Spit it out."

Terrance flinched like a frightened dog. "It's gold, sir. A hundred-pound nugget of pure gold, and I know just where to find it."

CHAPTER 47

"Mr. Martin, Mr. Collins," Able Dean said when they met just inside *El Caballero*, "this is my fiancé, Miss Della Strand."

Clutching his hat to his abdomen, Heck gave a low nod. "Ma'am."

"Pleased to meet you, ma'am," Sam said.

"It's my pleasure," Miss Strand said. She was a plump, pretty, young lady with a bright smile and rosy cheeks framed by straw-colored curls. "Able tells me you gentlemen have come to us out of the very heart of the wilderness."

"Yes, ma'am," Heck said. "We're out there a way."

"Doesn't it get lonely?"

"No, ma'am. I'm married, and we have plenty of neighbors. We're starting a little town."

"Starting a town?" Miss Strand said, her eyes shining with interest. "That sounds downright adventurous, doesn't it, Able?"

Able Dean raised his brows. "On one hand, it sounds adventurous. But on the other—no offense, gentlemen—it sounds like a good way to get scalped."

"Well, there is that," Heck said with a grin.

Miss Strand's mouth dilated into a perfect O of surprise. "Oh my goodness! You don't have any trouble with Indians, do you?"

"Nothing we can't handle, ma'am," Heck said.

At that moment, the host came in, greeted them with a smile, checked their reservation, and told them to follow him.

As the man led them to their table, Heck began to feel uncomfortable.

Folks looked up at him as he passed. Their gazes lingered. He was used to people staring. Being six and a half feet tall tended to draw folks' attention.

But in the stares of these people, he read more than surprise over his stature.

This was a *very* fancy restaurant, the fanciest he'd been in since he fought in New Orleans and his boxing manager, Mr. Corcoran, had taken him to a hotel to meet a bunch of reporters fascinated by tales of a fifteen-year-old boy outboxing full-grown men.

Only in New Orleans, Mr. Corcoran had told Heck to wear a suit.

Here, Heck wore only the denim pants and light blue shirt Hope had made him. There nothing wrong with these clothes. They were clean and fit him well. But the other diners, including his companions, wore fine suits and expensive-looking gowns.

Most folks just glanced, lingered momentarily, then went

back to their meals and conversation. But several people stared and frowned, letting him know what they thought of his attire.

They walked into an adjacent room, and the host led them past other diners to a table in the corner.

At the center of the room, two tables had been shoved together. Men filled all the seats, staring toward the head of the table, where a huge man with a crumpled nose roared, "I hit him so hard with the left, he begged for the right!" Then he burst into loud gales of laughter.

Most of the men at his table laughed boisterously, acting like they'd never heard anything half so funny. A few at the far end scribbled madly, reminding Heck of the reporters he had just been remembering.

Heck and Sam stood while Able Dean pulled out the chair for his fiancé.

Once Miss Strand was settled, the men took their seats. Heck sat with his back to the wall. Over Miss Strand's shoulder, he could see the bellowing ox of a man at the central table.

"So I says to the crowd, I says, *that's* how the champion of the West does it!" The man pounded a big fist on the table, rattling the dishes, and gulped down a tankard as the sycophants laughed and the reporters scribbled.

This big, loud man was claiming to be the champion of the West—the exact title Heck had won three years earlier as a fifteen-year-old boy in St. Louis.

Something rose in Heck then, something like a growl rising in the throat of a perturbed dog... and with it came questions.

Who was this man?

Did he really hold the title?

If Heck had stayed in the sport, could he have beaten this enormous man?

But as quickly as these questions occurred to him, Heck rejected them. Those days were over. Long over.

Boxing was part of his boyhood. A thing he had taken seriously for a while, a thing that had been very good to him, thanks to the prize money and the incredible amounts of cash people were always willing to bet against him.

But yes, those days were over.

He realized Able Dean had spoken to him.

"I'm sorry, sir," Heck said. "I was distracted. Could you repeat that, please?"

Able Dean leaned closer and kept his voice low. "That man over there—against the wall—the lean man with the drooping, silver mustache?"

Heck nodded, seeing the man. He was well-dressed and wore a pistol on his hip. His pant legs had hiked up a bit, revealing a good portion of the most beautiful boots Heck had ever seen.

"That is *Don* Vasquez," Able Dean said with a smile, "one of the men interested in your auction."

Heck observed the man with renewed interest. "You don't say."

"What a splendid coincidence," Miss Strand said. "What will you be auctioning, cattle? I know *Don* Vasquez is one of the wealthiest ranchers in the country."

"What Mr. Martin will be auctioning is a private matter, my dear," Able Dean said gently.

"Oh, I am so sorry," Miss Strand said, blushing. "I didn't mean to intrude. I am so very sorry if I offended you, Mr.

Martin."

Heck laughed. "Ma'am, I don't reckon I've ever been offended in my whole life. And I know where you're coming from. I've always had a pronounced sense of curiosity myself."

This seemed to make Miss Strand feel better.

"Just like I told these two ladies afore we come here," the big man at the center table bellowed. "You're looking at none other than Big Jess Heller, the champion of the West, and if you two birds want to walk again this week, you'd best bring in a couple more sweeties to lend a hand."

Laughter erupted around the table.

Elsewhere in the room, folks looked uncomfortable.

Able Dean either hadn't heard the lout or was ignoring him. "Here comes *Don* Vasquez," the lawyer said, smiling and waving to the approaching rancher. "He's a good man who's built a cattle empire here, a strong potential buyer."

Apparently, *Don* Vasquez had not allowed his money to soften him. Though middle-aged, the man was lean and looked hard as nails. Based on his tanned, leathery face and bowlegged gait, he had spent a good deal of time atop a horse.

Heck and the other men rose.

Able Dean made the introductions.

Vasquez's handshake was firm. He looked Heck directly in the eyes.

Then, the *don* bowed deeply and kissed the hand of Miss Strand. There was nothing inappropriate in his action, only a politely flattering gesture from a Spanish gentleman.

When *Don* Vasquez realized that Heck was the owner of the nugget—or as Able Dean put it, "the artifact"—the rancher simply smiled, his eyes twinkling with interest, and said he looked forward to the auction.

Then, as the big man at the center table hollered for the waiter to bring him more beer, *Don* Vasquez winced slightly. His lips curled slightly in a dangerous smile. "A man like that needs a lesson. Unfortunately, San Franciscans frown on shooting people at supper."

They chuckled at his dark humor and bade him farewell.

Heck happened to agree with the man. What right did this big, so-called champion of the West have to ruin everyone's meal?

Heck wanted to tell the guy to mind his manners but resolved to hold his tongue. After all, this was a nice restaurant, and he was out with nice people. He didn't want Miss Strand to think him a savage.

But then Big Jess Heller said something Heck couldn't ignore.

"Mmm," he said loudly, staring at Miss Strand, "there's a nice ripe little bird. I'd like to pluck her feathers."

Miss Strand gasped.

Able Dean snarled. His face turned red. But instead of turning toward the rude giant, he clasped his fiancé's hand comfortingly.

Heck, however, couldn't let it stand. He stood and pointed. "You watch your mouth."

Heller shot to his feet. He was nearly as tall as Heck and much thicker. He had a heavy brow and cruel eyes, and his ears were as crumpled as his nose. In his haste, he knocked over his tankard.

For a few seconds, he just stood there, staring daggers at Heck.

The room around them quivered. In the tense silence, the sound of the spilled beer running off the table and hitting the floor was very loud.

"Are you talking to me?" Heller asked.

"Yes, I am. And I'll say it once more, so you hear me clearly. Watch. Your. Mouth."

The giant looked at his friends and laughed loudly. At the opposite end of the table, reporters scribbled frantically.

Heller's laughter cut off abruptly, and he stared at Heck again, stabbing the air between them with a fat finger. "You got no idea who you're sassing, boy. I'm Big Jess Heller, the—"

"That's another thing," Heck said, cutting him off. "Where did you get that title, the champion of the West?"

Heller puffed out his chest. "I won it. In the ring, boy. With these."

He held up his huge fists as if they might scare Heck.

"Who did you beat?" Heck asked.

"Mighty Paul Branson. Though he wasn't so mighty after he felt my power." Heller again turned to his friends, and they had another laugh together.

"And who did he beat?"

"Lots of people. He didn't get the name Mighty for nothing."

"But who had the title before him?"

"Some kid." Heller shifted his eyes to Miss Strand. "Now, what do you say, little lady? Do you want to come over here and join a real man for supper?"

Miss Strand gasped again.

"I warned you," Heck said.

"What are you going to do, shoot me? You'd better kill me with the first shot, or I'll shove that six-shooter—"

"No, I'm gonna whip you with my fists," Heck declared.

"You?!" Heller threw back his big head with wild laughter. "You're a matchstick. I'd snap you in half."

"Want to put some money on it?" Heck asked, staring back at him.

"You can't be serious."

"Oh, I'm serious," Heck said. His quick mind had been working this whole time, and he suddenly recognized an opportunity to make real money. "I'll bet any amount you want."

"Get out of here, kid. You're fixing to get yourself hurt."

"I'll cut you to ribbons and bust your ribs, and you'll quit in the ring."

"In the ring, is it?" Heller boomed laughter again. "Keep your dollar, kid."

"How about three thousand dollars?"

All around the room, people inhaled sharply.

Heller grinned, suddenly interested. "You have three thousand dollars? Three thousand dollars that you'll wager that you can beat me, Big Jess Heller, the champion of the West?"

"That's right," Heck said. "In a ring, with a referee and a crowd... with your title on the line."

The reporters were fiercely attentive, scribbling madly as their eyes flicked back and forth between the men.

One of the men at the table stood and addressed Heck. "My name is Newsome. I'm Mr. Heller's manager. Young man, if you will agree to shave your beard and put your challenge in writing, we will accept your offer on the spot, and we can have a fight in three days' time."

"A fight's not enough," Heck said. "Can you have the money, too?"

Mr. Newsome nodded, looking amused. "Yes, we can have the money."

"All right, because you're gonna need it."

Heller laughed again. "This is gonna be the easiest payday I ever had!"

By Mr. Newsome's unpleasant smile, he apparently agreed. "What's your name, young man?"

Heck told him, but having thought things through, he pronounced his name the way Mexicans had back in Taos, making it sound like *Ector Marteen*.

"All right, Mr. Martín. When can you sign a contract and deliver the money to an agreed-upon guarantor?"

"Tomorrow morning, first thing."

"Excellent," Newsome said. "Let's plan on having the fight on Friday, four days from now. That will give us time to spread the word."

"Yeah," Heller laughed, "and give you time to draw up your last will and testament!"

Both parties were seated again.

Some of the reporters came over and started peppering Heck with questions, but he waved them off and said only, "I'm stronger than I look. I've been in a few fights before, and I've never lost."

"Yes, Mr. Martín," one of the reporters said, "but have you ever boxed before?"

"Once the punches start flying, what difference does it make?" Heck said, evading the question. "I'm gonna teach him to mind his manners."

"Can we give you a ring name, Mr. Martín? It'll help get folks excited. What do you want us to call you?"

"Well, since I'm a gentleman teaching this fellow to be polite, you can call me *El Caballero*."

This seemed to please the reporters, whom Heck dismissed, saying that he wanted to eat his meal in peace.

Sam grinned at him.

Able Dean and his fiancé looked horrified.

"Surely, you're not going to follow through with this?" Miss Strand said.

"As your attorney," Able Dean said, "I assure you that no court would hold you responsible for the money at this point. But if you actually sign a contract…"

"I'm gonna sign the contract," Heck said.

"But then you're going to have to fight him."

"That's the point."

"Have you ever boxed before?" Miss Strand asked.

Heck nodded and whispered, "In fact, you know how he mentioned some kid holding the title before? That kid was me. I was fifteen."

The two fiancés looked shocked. "You?" they chorused.

"Yup, me. But don't go telling anybody. I want folks in San Francisco to think I'm just some yokel with a lot of money and an outsized notion of his own abilities. That way the betting odds will swing heavily in Heller's favor. Mr. Dean, can you arrange a number of bets on my behalf?"

"You're not thinking of betting on him and throwing the fight?" Able Dean said.

"Not in a million years. No, I'm betting on myself and

hoping you can set up someone to field big wagers against my money."

"How much?"

"Eleven thousand dollars if the odds go as high as I expect they will."

CHAPTER 48

Heck picked up the ridiculous restaurant tab, parted ways with Able Dean and Miss Strand, then walked with Sam back to the shabby boarding house they'd found on the waterfront.

Darkness had transformed San Francisco.

The streets were emptier than they had been, but a lot of rough-looking men loitered in front of shops and at the mouths of alleys. Many called out, offering illicit pleasures for sale.

Heck and Sam marched steadily forward, keeping watchful eyes.

The streets reeked with sin, and menace filled the air. Drunks stumbled everywhere, mostly in the form of mustachioed packs who laughed and shouted, shoved and stumbled.

Heck avoided eye contact. The last thing he needed now was to get into a fight. Not only might he break a knuckle or take a knife to the back, hurting his chances in Saturday's fight, but also someone might see him put the knuckles to a few miners and start talking once the word of his match with Heller spread.

That sort of thing might skew the odds unfavorably. Folks would still bet against him, but he wanted the best odds he could get.

"You really think you can beat him?" Sam asked as they strode along.

Heck nodded. "Otherwise, I wouldn't take the fight, let alone bet all of my money."

"He's a big fella."

"That he is. But a lot of the men I fought were big."

"As big as him?"

"His size doesn't bother me. It's just a fact, something I can't ignore. I'd be a fool to stand in front of him and trade punches."

"So what will you do?"

"That big, bony head and thick neck, I don't think I can knock him out, so I'll do just what I told him. Cut him to ribbons, break his ribs, and make him quit."

"Better you than me, my friend. He looks like he hits very hard."

"I'm sure he does. But I'm not just going to stand there and let him wail on me. I'm going to use my head. To tell you the truth, the thing that concerns me isn't his size or power. It's his nose and ears."

"They looked pretty mangled."

"Exactly. Which means he's been around. Some big guys come in and win a few fights easily, relying solely on their size and strength, and never really learn anything. But Heller has clearly been through some wars. That means he's likely got some tricks up his sleeve."

"Like Mr. Dean said, it's not too late to pull out."

"And like I told Mr. Dean, there's no way I'm pulling out. This fight is a huge opportunity for me. Besides, somebody really needs to shut Heller's mouth. He's rude and obnoxious, and he was impolite to Miss Strand."

Sam nodded. "Knock some manners into him, Heck."

They walked in silence for a while.

Then, Sam said, "But if you haven't boxed in a couple of years, aren't you going to be out of shape?"

"Physically, I'm in great shape. In the last three years, I've gotten a lot bigger. Taller, longer reach, more muscle. Stronger, too. It's not like I've been sitting around knitting."

"No, you've been working in the wilderness and killing grizzlies with a Bowie knife."

Heck chuckled. "It's true, though. I'm physically and psychologically ready to tear this giant apart. The only problem is my timing and movement and combinations. I haven't thrown punches in years. The next few days, I'll try to get my footwork and combinations back. Then, during the fight, I'll be extra cautious the first few rounds. Mostly move and jab. Stay away from his big punches. Then, as I get my rhythm back, I'll start picking things up."

"And around then, he'll start to understand that he's made a big mistake."

"That's right," Heck said.

They had reached their boarding house and were walking down the hall to their room. "You'll be there. Watch for the moment. You'll see it in his eyes and maybe in his body, too. Watch for the moment when his will breaks and he realizes he's made a terrible mistake."

Heck pulled out the key as they reached the door, but there was no reason to use it.

The door was open. Not just ajar. Busted from its hinges.

Heck pulled his pistol. Sam pulled his derringer.

Heck stood there, listening for a moment, heard nothing, and pushed into the room.

No one was there.

But someone obviously had been.

By the shaft of moonlight falling through the window, Heck could see his room had been completely trashed.

Someone had broken in and gone through everything. Their cots were overturned, the sheets torn off, the mattresses gutted. Their bags had been emptied on the floor. Someone had even pried up floorboards and knocked holes in the wall.

Heck lit a lamp and brought the chaos into clearer view. "They stole my Hawken," he growled, burning with rage. He'd had that rifle since he was fifteen.

"And my rifle," Sam said and shook his fist. "This town is a cesspool!"

"Agreed," Heck said, but as his eyes scanned the destruction, his mind galloped ahead. "But this wasn't the work of random thieves."

"Why do you say that?"

Heck gestured toward the hall. "None of those rooms were broken into. And look at what the thieves did here. This was no quick, clumsy burglary. They were hunting for something."

"You think somebody was looking for..."

"I do. Why else tear everything apart this way? Look, they even tore up floorboards over there."

"Do you think Able Dean would..."

Heck shook his head. "My gut says no. He's got a good thing going and stands to make money from the deal as is. Plus he doesn't strike me as the type."

"One of the potential buyers, then?"

"I have no idea," Heck said, but in his mind, he recalled the sound of papers falling to the ground.

"I thought of something else," Sam said.

"What's that?"

"Why are none of our neighbors here? Or the man that runs this place? They had to hear something. But they're tucked away like rabbits."

"I guess they're afraid."

Sam nodded. "Which suggests that someone frightening did this."

"Probably a gang. Jim said the waterfront is loaded with them."

"Let's get out of here before they come back," Sam said.

"Good idea."

"And let's find a room on the other side of town."

Heck frowned at that. "I wish I could get a room across the street and keep an eye. I reckon they'll be back. But that would mean keeping watch all day and all night, and I'm gonna need my sleep before this fight."

"So let's cut our losses and cross town," Sam said, already inching toward the shattered doorway.

Heck agreed, but he was filled with bitterness. He wanted his Hawken back.

He would not forget it.

Maybe, just maybe, he would find a way to recover his trusty rifle... and punish those who'd stolen it.

CHAPTER 49

"There you are, sir," the barber said, holding up a mirror. "What do you think?"

Heck glanced at his reflection, rubbed a rough hand over the square jaw he hadn't seen in years, and nodded. "Looks like you did what I asked. I'm clean-shaven, and my hair's short."

"You look a lot different, Heck," Sam said, after they paid and left. "Almost civilized."

"Yeah, well, don't let looks deceive you. I'm still the same old savage, beard or no beard."

He glanced out at the bay. As usual, it was packed with ships. How did they even maneuver with so many of them jammed in there?

Where there's a will, there's a way, he thought. And the folks who owned those boats stood to make a lot of money selling whatever cargo they were carrying.

He and Sam had spent a rough night in a waterfront dive, sleeping on a floor among more than a dozen other men. The place was filthy, and the smells and snoring were unbearable. Heck had slept with his sheathed Bowie in one hand in case anyone tried to rob or Shanghai him, but no one had been so stupid.

This sort of sleeping arrangement was common here. Most miners slept in tents or twenty to a room in dirty conditions.

Yes, some were striking gold, but all of them were getting fleeced. The only people getting rich were the merchants upon whom the miners depended for the basics of life. One enterprising woman was said to have made $18,000 selling pies in the minefields.

"Well, I certainly hope we never have to spend another night like that," Sam said, looking bleary-eyed as they continued their trek across town.

They had decided to check into one of the fancy hotels far from the waterfront, though after paying over a hundred dollars for supper the previous night, Heck hated to think what a room would cost.

"Come on," Heck said, taking a detour. "I want to stop in and see Able Dean."

"You going to tell him what his clerk did?"

"We can't be certain he's the guilty party. But I'm gonna warn Mr. Dean of our suspicions and be awful careful what I share in Terrance's hearing."

When they went through the door, Terrance popped up, wearing another expensive-looking suit and a nervous smile. "Good morning, sirs. Mr. Martin, I barely recognized you without your beard."

Heck nodded. "Morning, Terrance. Is Mr. Dean in?"

"Not at the moment, sir. Would you care to leave a message?"

"No thanks. When do you expect him to return?"

"I'm not sure, sir. It might be a while. Are you sure you wouldn't like to leave a message?"

"I'm positive," Heck said and leaned against the wall, where he could keep an eye on both Terrance and the door.

"Is everything all right, sir?" Terrance asked, looking more nervous than ever.

Heck nodded and crossed his arms over his chest. "Waiting."

"Yes, sir. Well, if you change your mind—"

"I won't."

"All right, sir."

Five minutes later, Able Dean walked through the door.

He stopped dead in his tracks and smiled. "Great Scott, you're clean-shaven, Mr. Martin. You look young and..."

"Civilized?" Sam offered.

Mr. Dean spread his hands. "Well, you look handsome, Mr. Martin, and ready to fight."

"I'll be ready."

"Excellent. I'm just returning from setting up our man in town. Once you give me however much money you want to wager, I'll get it to him, and he'll start accepting bets on your behalf. He wants fifteen percent."

That was a ridiculous sum—ten percent was standard—but Heck nodded. "Done. I'll have the money for you soon."

"Outstanding. And later today, I'll be having lunch with Mr. Newsome. We'll be drawing up the contracts. If you'd like to join us, we could get everything signed. Apparently, he already had a venue in place for an exhibition. Heller was going to draw a big crowd, run through a series of supposedly tough miners, then pocket half the gate money and head home. He's getting flyers printed. He'll ask us to split the cost."

"Are we getting a cut of the gate?" Heck asked.

"I doubt it."

"Then he can pay for the flyers and all publicity. I'll put up my money and show up Saturday night. Winner takes all. I'm not playing business games with him."

Mr. Dean nodded. "What about lunch?"

"Can't make it," Heck said. "I'll sign soon, though."

"That's fine," Mr. Dean said. "Come on over to my desk, and I'll show you the contract, anyway."

The three of them went over, and as Mr. Dean retrieved the contract, Heck grabbed a pen and paper and wrote, *I need to share some things with you privately. Don't say anything aloud. I don't want your clerk to hear. I'll continue to write on this paper.*

He shoved his message across the desk.

Mr. Able saw it, read the words quickly, glanced toward his clerk's back, and nodded. "All right, Mr. Martin," he said aloud, handing Heck the contract and the sheet of paper, "here's the contract. Please take your time reading it and let me know if you have any questions."

"Thank you, sir," Heck said and instead of reading the contract, wrote out his account of what had happened, his suspicions about Terrance, and how he wanted to handle things.

Once he'd finished this, he handed the note to Mr. Dean and went through the contract, which seemed clear and simple and fair to him.

There was an opportunity to negotiate for a percentage of

the tickets sold, but with such short notice and no real leverage, he didn't want to risk jeopardizing the fight.

Besides, if he started looking too savvy, Newsome might start to wonder who he really was. If word got out among the town's power brokers that Newsome was fleecing this overconfident mountain man, it could only help skew the odds.

Mr. Dean handed him a slip of paper that read, *I am terribly sorry for your difficulties, Mr. Martin. I can't imagine Terrance doing such a thing—he's the son of an old friend—but I will exercise the greatest caution around him and all others. I will do as you have indicated and meet you at four o'clock at the intersection you indicated, and yes, I will take care to ensure that I am not followed.*

"This looks good, Mr. Dean," Heck said, handing him the contract. "I'll stop by here again tomorrow at noon and sign everything then if they approve the terms and sign today."

Mr. Dean, who folded up their real plans and tucked them into his shirt pocket, shook Heck's hand and said, "Sounds like a plan, Mr. Martin."

CHAPTER 50

Heck spotted the two men as soon as he left Able Dean's office.

He registered their appearances and mannerisms then looked away and continued up the street.

They were a pair of short, stocky thugs in filthy coats that could be hiding anything.

For Heck, who'd been surviving on awareness for years, they had stuck out instantly, especially because they'd made it so obvious, one elbowing the other and pointing from across the street, where they instantly started drifting northward, obviously meaning to flank Heck.

Were there others, too?

Heck doubted it. This pair had been so clumsy, he was sure they would have signaled or at least glanced in the direction of other crewmembers.

Another reason he'd picked them up so easily was because he'd been expecting something like this. After all, if Terrance really was the informant, whoever was behind all this would assume that Heck had left the boarding house for good. His only hope at this point would be more news from Terrance—or to spot a very tall man coming out of Able Dean's office.

"Change in plans," Heck told Sam without breaking stride.

"What's that?"

"We're not heading straight to the hotel."

"Okay. Where do you want to go?"

"We'll just keep walking for a bit until we come to a street that isn't so crowded. Then we'll turn into an alley. That ought to get them excited."

"Get who excited?"

"Don't look, but two men across the street are following us."

"You're certain?"

"Certain."

"All right. What are we going to do?"

Heck told him.

They continued up the street, turned a corner, and started uphill. "Look out at the bay when I tell you to turn around," Heck said. "Don't look at the men."

"All right."

Heck glanced over his shoulder, hesitated, tapped Sam's shoulder, and stopped, pointing out at the bay and smiling.

Then, they turned around and continued uphill, Heck happy to see this street was less crowded than the last.

The men were still following them, of course, staying a bit behind them. They remained on the opposite side of the street for now, reminding Heck of other tails he'd picked up back in St. Louis, when he first learned about men like these.

He explained everything to Sam, adding, "I just wanted to

make sure they hadn't switched sides and moved up quickly behind us. I don't expect them to do anything that obvious, not in this area, but pinning your survival on assumptions is a great way to get killed. Hey, change in plans. Let's step in here for a moment."

Heck opened the door to a bookstore and went inside.

"You sure are in a changeable mood, my friend," Sam said.

"Flexibility and unpredictability are good ways to *avoid* getting killed," Heck said, then pretended to glance at the books in the window.

The men had stopped on the opposite side of the street and were talking now and looking in the direction of the bookstore.

"Good morning, gentlemen," a well-dressed man said, coming over to them. "Are you looking for any titles in particular?"

"Just browsing, thanks," Heck said.

"Take your time," the man said. "I apologize for my limited stock. This summer, I am supposed to receive another shipment, but you know how that goes."

Heck glanced out the window. They were still out there, half-watching the door.

Sam, who'd picked up a Charles Dickens novel, grunted with surprise. "Fifty dollars for a book?"

The man smiled sadly and nodded. "Yes, it's all a matter of supply and demand, I'm afraid. With so few women in town, most men turn to alcohol and gambling. Those who don't, turn to books."

"But fifty dollars?" Sam asked incredulously. "Just because you can get the money doesn't mean you should."

The man's smile went from sad to patient. "Sir, I am assuming you are new to town."

Sam nodded.

"After a few days here, you'll understand that if I wish to eat and keep a roof over my head, I need to sell these books for fifty dollars. You have entered a strange land, my friends, a land where everything is gold and greed, a land where nothing seems quite real, except, perhaps for a pleasant fantasy trapped between the covers of a good book."

"Well, happy reading, sir," Heck said. Then, to Sam, he said, "Let's go."

Back out on the street, he didn't bother even glancing at the men. He knew they were still there, just as he knew they would follow.

That had been the true purpose of the bookstore detour. To eliminate any chance that these men might be following out of coincidence.

With that possibility eliminated, Heck would now feel okay, handling things the way he knew they must be handled.

As they continued uphill, the number of people on the streets grew fewer still. They were skirting the burnt edge of the devastation left by the fire.

The men would look to make their move soon.

So Heck made his first.

"Hard right turn into this alley," he told Sam and slipped between two scorched buildings.

Once they were out of sight of the men, he ran.

Reaching the intersection with another alley, Heck took a sharp right and filled his fists with his Colt and Bowie.

As directed, Sam stood behind him, derringer at the ready in case Heck couldn't handle the situation on his own.

A moment later, Heck heard heavy footfalls and a faint jingling sound as the men charged up the alley after them.

As the first man came into view, pistol in hand, Heck smashed him in the forehead with the butt of his Bowie.

While the man collapsed to the ground, Heck swung his Colt on the other man, who lifted his own pistol, his eyes feral and desperate.

Heck shot him in the chest. The man fell beside his accomplice, who groggily patted the ground for his own firearm.

"Leave it," Heck warned him, but the man seized the gun and rolled, trying to get a shot—but got shot instead, when Heck pulled the trigger and ended the man, filling the alley once more with a tremendous roar.

The man with the chest wound cursed then moaned, "You done killed me, mister."

Heck crouched down and stared into the man's eyes. "Well, it's not too late to make peace with your maker."

The man nodded, wincing.

"Who sent you?" Heck demanded. "And remember, God hates liars. This is your chance to show a change of heart."

The man started to curse again, seemed to think better of it, and opened his eyes, grimacing in pain. "Getty," he gasped. "Bill Getty."

With that, he died.

"Let's get out of here," Sam said, clearly rattled by the skirmish. "You made an awful racket. People are sure to come running."

Heck nodded. "Just a second," he said, picking up and pocketing the men's firearms, then rifling quickly through their pockets.

"Heck, come on," Sam said, sounding frantic.

Holding up a handful of double eagles, Heck grinned at his worried friend. "I knew I heard jingling. These good men just paid for our lunch."

CHAPTER 51

Heck shuffled alongside the dusty trail, throwing
punches. His muscles felt strong but tight.

He threw a jab, dipped an invisible haymaker, and jabbed
again as he pivoted to safety.

The sun was sinking lower in the sky. In a couple of hours, it
would melt into the ocean.

Behind him, flames crackled and bacon sizzled as Sam fixed
everyone's supper.

It had been quite a day.

After escaping the alley, they had cut across the city to a
fancy brick hotel, where they learned a room would cost three
hundred dollars a night—or, in other words, nearly a year's
wages for most folks in the nation.

Needless to say, Heck was not going to pay that money.
Even if he'd had a million dollars, he wouldn't.

So they returned yet again to the center of town, where they
found a livery and bought a pair of riding horses for two

hundred dollars apiece—an exorbitant price but a seeming bargain for this town.

Once the transaction was finished, Heck said as much to the hostler.

The man shrugged. "Ain't much call for riding horses in these parts. Most folks want mules."

They rode the new horses out of town, stopping and watching from time to time to make sure no one was on their back trail.

No one followed them as they rode out of town, traveled a few miles, and returned to the camp where Jim Bridger and Two Bits had been staying.

When they explained everything that had happened, Jim Bridger was offended. "I've heard of that man, Getty. He's the blood money king. Sells more folks into servitude than any other. Meanwhile, he runs a clothing store in town."

Two Bits had picked up his rifle. "Go to store and kill?"

"Your call, Heck," Jim said. "You want to go down there and take care of business?"

"Thanks, Jim, but no. I just want to steer clear of Getty. I have too much riding on this fight, and if what you're saying is right, I'm sure Getty has bodyguards. Some of us might end up getting hurt."

Jim shrugged. "All right. You change your mind, say the word."

Heck retrieved his money from the iron box and returned to town, where he met Able Dean, who had the contract and news for him.

Heck signed and listened as Mr. Dean said, "The venue's set and the flyers are printed. Newsome's people are out in the camps, spreading the word. They're handling all the publicity."

"And getting all the gate."

Mr. Dean smiled and shook his head. "You're getting ten percent... if you win."

Heck grinned. "Nice work."

"A good lawyer does more than draw up contracts, Mr. Martin. Meanwhile, we have four potential buyers for the nugget. The earliest they can all attend the auction is Saturday morning."

"Day after the fight, huh? That works."

"Yes, they've agreed to come to my office at nine in the morning."

Heck shook his head. "Change in plans. We're gonna hold the auction someplace else."

"All right. Where?"

Heck told him.

Mr. Dean was surprised. "That's a strange place to hold an auction."

"It is, but it's where we're gonna hold it. Don't tell them yet. Don't tell anyone. Tell them the location will be provided by messenger early Saturday morning. Can you do that?"

"Certainly. And I applaud your caution. Speaking of which, I'm terribly sorry if—"

"He's guilty," Heck said. "I'm almost positive it was Terrance."

Mr. Dean frowned. "How do you know?"

Heck told him what had happened after he'd left the office.

Mr. Dean was horrified. "I'm so glad you're all right. And Sam?"

"Sam's fine. A little rattled but unscathed. The thugs worked for a man called Getty."

"Bill Getty," Mr. Dean said, nodding. "A notorious scoundrel. I am so sorry that my employee dragged you into this mess. I will report Terrance to the police, of course. It will break his parents' hearts, but I must do it."

"Agreed," Heck said. "He's a menace. But Mr. Dean, do me a favor, and don't turn him in until after I'm safely out of town."

"Of course. You're wise not to let Getty know how much you know."

"Speaking of getting home," Heck said, "I'm expecting more trouble from Getty after the fight, so I'm going home by a different route. I'm wondering if you can help me arrange transportation."

"Of course, sir. Anything."

So Heck had paid those estimated costs, increased Dean's retainer, and handed over eleven thousand dollars to be wagered on Heck, who advised Mr. Dean again to hold off on opening those bets until the odds looked good.

"I expect them to start somewhere around two to one," Heck said, remembering the pattern of his many fights in the past. "Then, when the bets flood in for Heller, the odds will shoot up. They'll probably peak tomorrow. After that, a few folks will start pinning their hopes on me, and the odds will fall back down a little. The minute they start dropping, open the bets."

Leaving Mr. Dean, Heck once again rode out of town, careful, of course, to watch his back trail.

Now, back among his friends, the only people here that he really trusted, Heck shuffled and dipped and punched. His body was warming up, remembering its old tricks.

But if he hoped to beat this monster Heller, he was going to have to loosen up by Friday night.

One thing, though. He'd matured a lot between his fifteenth and eighteenth year. He wasn't just taller and broader and more muscular. His bones were bigger, thicker, heavier, and his muscles were hard as iron.

He'd always had a good punch. In fact, even at fifteen, he had knocked out all twenty of his opponents. But he had never faced such a thick-necked bull of a man as Heller.

Heck ripped a hard combination—jab, right cross, left hook, right uppercut—slashing and battering his invisible opponent. His explosiveness surprised him.

Just exactly how much power had he gained?

"You hit him with an uppercut like that, he'll land in the bay," Jim laughed.

Beside him, Two Bits offered a rare smile, clearly appreciating Heck's display.

Jim patted his money belt. "I'm betting a thousand dollars on you, my friend."

CHAPTER 52

"Where has he gone?" Bill Getty demanded.

The cluster of men clotting the alley behind his haberdashery grunted and shrugged and looked at their muddy feet, most of which were bare.

"Nobody's seen nothing for days, boss," one said.

"How does a man of his height simply disappear?"

"Maybe he's staying on a boat?" one of the men hazarded.

Getty turned to Leo, his personal bodyguard and sergeant-at-arms. "I thought you said you checked the water."

"We did, boss. The floating hotels, anyway."

"Expand the search," Getty said. "Get some men in rowboats tonight. Go from vessel to vessel. Start with those you know. Ask if they've seen a tall man."

"Okay, boss."

"Sir?" one of the younger men whose name Getty couldn't remember said.

"What is it?"

"Why not just wait for the night of the fight? We know where he'll be then."

"No," Getty said.

Getty didn't snap it, though, because at least the kid was thinking logically, which was more than he could say for most of his goons. Maybe this kid had the brains to become an asset. Or a threat. Either way, he was worth keeping an eye on.

"The night of the fight," Getty said, "he'll be surrounded by well-wishers. Especially before he gets stomped in the ring. Then, afterward, he'll lose everything."

"Not the nugget, though, right, Mr. Getty?" the kid whose name he couldn't remember countered. "The auction's not until Saturday morning, right?"

"Right, but if this Hector Martin is crazy enough to fight Heller, he's also crazy enough to bet the nugget on himself, auction or no auction. He must be soft in the head. Heller's a killer, a certified killer. How many men has he killed in the ring, Leo?"

"Three, boss. Well, two in the ring. The other one hung on for a few days."

"Yes, and then he died," Getty said. "That's my point. Heller only has what, a dozen fights? He's killed a quarter of his opponents. This kid has slim chances of surviving and zero chance of winning. Which is why he's a fifteen-to-one favorite now. Luckily, I understood the situation early on, when the odds were only five to one, and put down a nice, fat bet on Mr. Heller."

In truth, it had been more than a fat bet. He'd wagered every bit of free capital on Heller—a touch over seventeen thousand dollars—which meant Friday night, he'd be three thousand four hundred dollars richer.

Which would be nice.

But what he really wanted was that nugget. A hundred pounds of pure gold…

Even melted into ingots, that would bring him twenty-five thousand dollars.

That was enough money, if he liquidated his considerable assets here, to head back to New York City and live like a king for the rest of his days.

So yes, he wanted the nugget. It was, in the language of the streets, the score of a lifetime.

"Get out there and find him, or I'll have your heads," Getty said, and stormed back into his shop with the shotgun-toting Leo at his heels.

Marcel, his part-time salesman, was helping a customer.

"Good day, sir," Getty said, strolling into the main room—and instantly filled with bile for having shown such respect because this was no customer.

"Hello, Mr. Getty," the sniveling law clerk said.

"What is it, Terrance? I'm a busy man. So far, your hot tip has brought me nothing but trouble."

"I'm sorry, sir, but I do bring important information."

"Don't just stand there trembling like a little girl. What is it?"

"Mr. Martin."

"What about him?"

"Mr. Dean had me make a booking for him."

Getty smiled. "What hotel?"

"Not a hotel, sir. A boat. He's booked passage for his home trip. He lives a thousand miles east of here in the wilderness.

Apparently, he's decided to take a ship from here to Oregon and take the upper trail home."

"That's too late, you idiot. I want the nugget now. Find out where he's staying now."

Terrance flinched. "I'm sorry, sir. I've been trying. I'll keep trying. But I just thought… Sorry, sir." He started to back away.

"Where do you think you're going?" Getty demanded.

"B-b-back to work, sir," Terrance stammered. "Thought you wanted me to—"

"Tell me about this booking. The boat, the time, the cabin number if you have it."

Terrance smiled weakly, making Getty want to pick him up by the ankles and dash his brains out on the floor. "Yes, sir, I have all that, even the cabin number, sir."

"Well, then, give it all to me," Getty demanded. He hoped to seize the nugget before the fight, of course, but if all else failed and Martin somehow managed to survive Friday night's contest, at least this booking would give Getty another shot.

On a boat, there's nowhere to hide and nowhere to run.

CHAPTER 53

"Weighing in at two hundred and thirty pounds and standing six feet, seven inches tall, with a record of zero wins, zero losses, and zero draws—but, he assures us, a lot of fights won against savage brutes in the wilderness—a genuine mountain man, Hector 'El Caballero' Martín!"

The crowd erupted with raucous cheering, which came as no surprise to Heck, since most of them expected to make money while watching him get crushed by his hulking opponent.

Also unsurprising to Heck was the way the betting odds had fluctuated, peaking at seventeen-to-one before plummeting over the last several hours to a neat and tidy ten-to-one.

Before the fight, Able Dean had reported the happy news that his man had secured sixteen-to-one odds.

Mr. Dean had brought additional happy news as well. The fairgrounds teemed with humanity, drunken men packed in on all sides, most of San Francisco's population having shown up to watch Heller crush him.

Mr. Dean estimated the crowd at over twenty thousand men. Since Newsome was charging an astonishing ten dollars a head, that meant the fight was bringing in two hundred thousand dollars, ten percent of which belonged to Heck... if he won.

The size of the crowd was a surprise to Heck. Never, in all of his twenty professional fights, had he fought before a crowd anywhere close to this size. The shouting spectators spread out in all directions as far as he could see—despite the unthinkable ticket price of ten dollars.

But then again, these men were hauling gold dust, paying a dollar for an unbuttered slice of bread, and no doubt starved for entertainment.

Well, Heck was fixing to give them just that.

The biggest surprise to him, however, was his own size. His height hadn't shocked him. Though he wouldn't have thought he was six-foot-seven, he had known that he'd grown taller.

The real shocker was his weight. Weighing in at two hundred and thirty pounds meant he was seventy pounds heavier than he'd been when, at fifteen, he'd first won the championship of the West.

"And across the ring," the small man with the big voice shouted, "hailing from New Orleans, Louisiana, tipping the scales at a powerful three hundred and five pounds, with a perfect record of twelve fights, zero defeats, and zero draws, all twelve fights coming by way of knockout, the heavyweight champion of the West, 'Big' Jess Heller!"

The crowd went absolutely wild. Here was the biggest, most

powerful, most famous man they had ever seen, the muscle-bound giant who'd killed three men with his punches and who was, they were sure, about to make them all a bit richer.

Heller roared, thrust his enormous fists into the air, and hopped up and down like some great, hairy ape. He was thick all over with legs like tree stumps and a big belly that wobbled beneath a barrel chest held up by broad, muscular shoulders from which hung the biggest arms Heck had ever seen. His chest and back and arms and legs were matted with dark fur.

Sneering at Heck, Heller pointed across the ring. "You're gonna be number four, big mouth!"

Heck said nothing in return. He'd learned a long time ago to let his fists do the talking. Besides, at this point Heller really believed Heck was just some overconfident woodsman in for the surprise of a lifetime.

That assumption was a weapon Heck planned to use against his massive opponent. It wouldn't last long. Once Heck started slipping punches and landing his own, Heller would realize that he had a real opponent in front of him. But there was no reason to cede that weapon until Heck had used Heller's ignorance against him.

Heck studied Heller for other weaknesses but found none. Beneath that big belly likely dwelled a stony abdomen. The flab around Heller's middle would just serve to pad and protect his ribs.

Heck hoped it would also slow the man and tire him as the fight dragged on. The excess weight might also affect his balance, though Heck figured Heller had probably carried it through his whole career.

The brevity of that career—twelve fights against Heck's

twenty—was another potential weakness, especially since most of Heller's fights ended in the first few rounds, as soon as he landed a clean punch on his opponents' jaws.

"He sure is big. Think it's too late to pull my bet?" Jim Bridger joked in Heck's corner.

"Gentlemen," the referee said, beckoning them to the center of the ring.

The massive crowd fell silent, crackling with anticipation and the fighters met for the stare down.

Heller stared up at Heck, eyes full of malice, nostrils flared, blowing like a horse.

He was trying to intimidate Heck, of course. Let him try.

Heck kept his eyes on the ref, who said, "We'll have a clean fight, do you understand, men? I know there's bad blood between you, but you must fight clean. And that means no butting, no elbows, no low blows. And I won't stand for any shenanigans, either. This is boxing, do you understand?"

He was mostly addressing Heck, which made sense, since none of these people had figured out yet who Heck really was.

"I said, do you understand?"

Heck nodded. "Yes, sir."

The ref turned to Heller. "And you, Mr. Heller?"

"Yeah, yeah, get on with it so I can smash his skull."

"No kicking, men," the ref said, "no rabbit punches, no punches to the kidneys, no biting. Do you hear me?"

"I don't need to fight dirty to snap him in half," Heller declared.

"And you, Mr. Martín, do you understand?"

Heck nodded.

They went back to the corners to await the opening bell.

The crowd murmured with excitement.

Jim Bridger leaned over the ropes to give Heck a sip of water from his canteen. "If I were you, Heck, I'd just shoot him."

Heck laughed. "They frown on that in boxing."

"Well, in that case—"

But whatever Jim had been going to say was lost by the ringing of the bell and the roar of the crowd as all three hundred and five pounds of Big Jess Heller came raising across the ring with one enormous fist cocked to the shoulder.

CHAPTER 54

Heck ducked the punch—barely—and spun away from the ropes as Heller charged after him.

Heck danced away into the relative safety of the center of the ring. He couldn't afford to get trapped against the ropes or, worse yet, in a corner by this power-punching monster.

Heller charged after him, pumping a lazy jab as a range finder and feinted, likely expecting Heck to overreact and create a fatal opening, but Heck didn't take the bait and circled away, easily evading Heller's right cross.

That's it, Heck told himself. *Take your time. You haven't done this for years. Let it come back to you. And let him get tired. This is the strongest his punches will be.*

In testament to that notion, Heller charged in again—he was quick for his size—and sliced the air with two sweeping hooks, a left and a right that Heck managed to slip under.

He saw the opening and knew he could land a clean shot on Heller's body—but to what effect... and at what cost?

So he let the opening pass and swiveled away again, retreating once more to the center of the ring.

"Fight, you coward!" Heller bellowed.

The massive crowd picked up the command, chanting, "Fight! Fight! Fight!"

Heck ignored them and continued to execute his plan, getting a sense of Heller and the ring and the tempo of the fight, its rhythm, its truth.

Minutes passed.

Heller continued to fight in bursts, charging and winging heavy shots, desperately annoyed that Heck wouldn't stand and fight like an idiot.

The crowd booed, demanding blood.

Heck hated them, as he had hated many crowds before in venues up and down the Mississippi.

Let them get in the ring and risk their lives.

He was here to win and secure a better life for his family, and against an opponent like this Goliath, that meant fighting intelligently.

His back touched the ropes, and he spun instantly away, retreating as reflexively as he would from a red-hot iron.

As the fight dragged on and the crowd grew more violent in its cursing and calls for blood, Heck felt his old rhythm coming back to him. With it came his sense of timing, a deadly weapon indeed.

As always, when faced with danger, his mind worked with incredible speed, slowing the world around him, and he evaded most of Heller's punches with relative ease.

A few, however, clipped him here and there, never cleanly, sending shivers all the way to his toes. One leaping hook grazed the side of his head, filling it with sparks.

Seconds later, Heck's eye swelled, narrowing his field of vision.

Which was dangerous. Because the punch you didn't see coming…

A buffalo rammed full speed into Heck's forehead. Everything erupted in bright light that sliced away into total darkness.

The next thing Heck knew, he was on his back, the noise of the crowd huge around him.

A blurry face leaned over him. Its mouth was moving.

"Six," the face said. "Seven…"

It was the ref.

"Eight…"

He was counting.

Counting Heck out…

CHAPTER 55

Heck struggled to his feet just in time. His legs wobbled beneath him.

Following the boxing rules of the age, the referee called a halt to the long first round and sent the men back to their corners for a thirty-second break.

The crowd shouted and laughed and jeered.

Heck staggered toward his corner, his head feeling like it was floating several inches above his body. His eye had swollen mostly shut.

Sam and Jim met him in the corner and gave him water.

They talked excitedly, but Heck didn't register their words. He shook his head, trying to clear the cobwebs filling his skull.

Across the ring, Heller was holding his fists in the air and gesturing to the crowd, getting them to chant his name louder and louder.

"Heller! Heller! Heller!"

Heck's head was clearing just as the ref called them back to their marks at the center of the ring.

Heck's legs felt strong again as he went to the center of the ring, but he knew he had to be extra careful now, knew Heller would look to finish this as soon as the bell rang, starting the second round.

Heller leered at him, eyes blazing with glee. "Gonna smash you now, boy! Gonna kill you!"

Heck shook out his arms and said nothing.

This was a fight for survival. A fight for Hope, a fight for his baby.

Whatever happened next, whatever Heck did, how he responded to this grim challenge… it would all become a story, a story his son or daughter would hear and learn, a part of the mythology of his or her father.

They would grow up knowing either that their father was knocked out in front of a crowd of thousands, battered and beaten by a better man, or that he had triumphed against the odds and conquered this huge opponent and for the second time won the heavyweight championship of the West.

And then, his son or daughter would make that story part of their own life, their own self-belief, reflecting on this moment as either a cautionary tale not to be like their father or as a source of strength that would help them through their own struggles in life.

The bell rang.

"Fight!" the ref shouted.

And Heck, more determined than ever, whipped a stiff jab into the face of his charging opponent and spun away at an angle, knowing he had to move, had to avoid unnecessary punishment, had to buy time to get his strength back and to sap the power of this murderous giant.

He barely ducked a furious haymaker that would have taken his head off.

"Getting closer, boy," Heller laughed. "Your eye ain't looking so good."

Heck said nothing and backpedaled to the center of the ring, vaguely aware of the jeering crowd urging Heller on.

They shouted all the louder as the pattern went on and on, minute after minute, Heck sticking and moving, choosing speed over power, keeping his attacker at bay and off-balance.

The spectators hated him for it.

Heck didn't care. He ignored them and focused instead on Heller's furry barrel chest, which was working in and out now like a fireplace billows. The big man's mouth hung sullenly open, sucking air.

The champion had clearly come to San Francisco expecting to plow through a pile of weak exhibition opponents. He wasn't in top shape, wasn't ready for an actual title fight. He probably hadn't even been training, and Heck had watched him gobble food and guzzle beer.

Heller still packed dangerous power in both hands, but he was huffing and puffing, and his feet plodded now rather than pounced.

They had been fighting for a long time. Since the knock-down, no one had been thrown to the canvas, knocked down, or fouled, so the ref hadn't called for a break in the action.

Heck felt strong again. And like a wolf seeing its prey stumble after a long chase across winter meadows, he filled with savage eagerness.

A frustrated Heller posed in front of him with his hands impatiently on his hips. "Come on, you coward—"

Heck walloped him with a lightning bolt right hand that caught the champion clean on the point of the chin and set him down on his butt.

The crowd roared with surprise, and the ref sent Heck to the neutral corner and started counting. The ref had been so shocked by the unexpected turn of events that several seconds elapsed before he even started counting, and yet the badly hurt Heller barely made it to his feet by the count of ten.

The ref called the round, and their thirty-second rest period began.

Jim Bridger slapped Heck's shoulder excitedly. "That's it, Heck! You really nailed him! He's hurt! Look at him shaking his head!"

"You're doing it, Heck!" Sam shouted, leaning over the ropes to squeeze Heck's sweaty arm. "You're really doing it!"

"Give me some water," Heck said, reminding his seconds of their duty.

"Sorry, Heck," Jim said and lifted the canteen to his lips.

Heck swished it around his mouth and spat into the bucket Sam was holding then took another sip and swallowed it. Not too much, though. He'd learned that lesson a long time ago.

Across the ring, Newsome was shouting at his hulking fighter and waving his towel up and down, fanning Heller's confused face, trying to get him more air. Another man held up a bottle. Heller grabbed it and chugged.

That's it, Heck thought, drink deep, *drink it all down.*

The bell rang, and this time Heck raced out of his corner, straight at the woozy giant.

Heller reacted like a warrior, hurling his hardest shot.

Just as Heck had expected.

Which is why, despite rushing wildly forward, Heck jolted to a stop just outside Heller's range.

Heller, still hurt from the knockdown, swung mightily, hit only the air, and slipped from the force of his own punch and fell to the ground.

The ref stepped between them, making sure Heck didn't hit the man while he was down.

But Heck wasn't interested in punching Heller at that moment. Instead, he employed a different weapon.

One benefit of not boasting or threatening during the buildup of a fight is reserving that right for a more precisely timed moment.

That moment was now.

"You know who I am now, don't you?" Heck called down to the big man crawling off the floor. "I'm him. I'm the kid."

Staggering to his feet, Heller spat blood and regarded Heck with confused belligerence. "What?"

The ref stepped away. "Box!"

Heck did not rush in and pummel his opponent, however. Yes, by holding back, he was giving Heller crucial seconds to recover his wits and become more dangerous; but Heck wanted to drive home this other, psychological attack first.

"I'm the kid who held the title. Not Hector Martín. Hector Martin. Heck Martin. The Mountain Man. I never lost. I just went away. And now I'm back for my title."

Heller's mouth dropped open with understanding.

Then Heck was on him, unloading with a heavy barrage that battered the big man back into the ropes. This whole time,

Heck had been holding back, letting Heller chase him and tire, but now Heck was a raging predator going for the kill. He pinned his opponent to the ropes and slammed through his weakening guard with punch after punch, throwing lefts and rights from full extension, turning his muscular shoulders with each blow so that his fists landed like hammer blows.

And what power his fist now held!

Heller's big head snapped backward on its thick neck, and his tree stump legs rotted beneath him, spilling him to the ground, this time for good.

As the crowd erupted with dismay, Heck threw his throbbing fists triumphantly into the air, knowing he was once more the heavyweight champion of the West... and, more importantly, the hero of a story that would someday bring strength to his child.

CHAPTER 56

The win was life-changing to say the least. And not just for Heck.

He had bet eleven thousand dollars on himself at sixteen-to-one odds. After subtracting fifteen percent for the betting agent and ten percent for Able Dean, he still won $132,000—an unthinkable fortune that he collected that night, along with the personal bet he'd made with Heller, who was surprisingly gracious in defeat.

"You know," Mr. Newsome said, as they were parting, "you could make a fortune in the ring and really cement your legacy. I'm certain I could arrange a fight with the heavyweight champion of the United States, Jerome Butler. Beating him would set you up to challenge for the world title against Mackey McGuinness."

"Right now, I just want to get home and see my wife and meet my baby for the first time," Heck said. "But if those men express interest in fighting me, just get in touch with Mr. Dean, and maybe we'll work something out."

The rest of the money, Heck's ten percent of the gate, would come to over $21,000 minus ten percent for Mr. Dean, who would collect and secure the earnings later this week after the venue did its accounting and made good on the purses.

Heck had advised Mr. Dean to invest that money as he best saw fit, trusting the man to make it grow.

They left Heller's hotel room with the upmost caution. Heck, Jim, Sam, Two Bits, and even Mr. Dean were armed and ready for trouble, but no one tried to rob or even follow them.

Which was a surprise. Heck had expected Getty to make a move.

But then again, both fighters and their teams had exited the fairgrounds as surreptitiously as possible before arriving at the hotel in the first place.

"Do you know how many acres you'd like to purchase now?" Mr. Dean asked Heck as they rode across town in his carriage.

Heck nodded and told him, laying out the parameters he wanted to purchase.

Mr. Dean and Sam Collins looked surprised.

Jim Bridger grinned. "Good move, Heck. Very smart move."

"Is there anything else you want me to take care of before you leave?" Mr. Dean asked Heck.

"There is one thing I'd really appreciate. I'd do it myself, but I want to steer clear of town as much as I can, and I'd love to have this thing before the auction tomorrow morning."

"Certainly," Mr. Dean said. "Anything. What would you like?"

"Rifles for Sam and me. This is the first time I've been without one for years. I feel vulnerable. And we'll be needing them for the long trip home."

"I will take care of that first thing in the morning," Mr. Dean said.

"Thank you. What are you fixing to do about Terrance?"

Mr. Dean sighed. "I was hoping you would write and sign a statement concerning his crimes. Once you've left town, I'll fire him and report everything to the police. I doubt the charges will stick, but I'm certain all of this will clip Terrance's wings. Then, I'll have the unpleasant business of writing to my old friend, his father. I loathe to do it, but it's my duty. After all, they deserve to know the truth, and Terrance is young enough that, with his parents' guidance, he still might make a man of himself."

Heck nodded, figuring that was a wise approach.

Then he eased back into his seat and blinked heavily, lulled by the hypnotic rhythm of the horses' hooves and the rocking of the carriage and the exhaustion which settled over him as heavily as a buffalo robe. His eye had swollen shut, his forehead throbbed from the big punch that had almost finished him, and his body ached the way it always did after a hard fight. His hands were stiff and sore to the wrists, the knuckles badly swollen and discolored.

But he'd done it. He'd won the title and the money and secured the valley and Hope City and a good future for his family.

All that remained now was the next morning's auction and whatever sum the nugget would bring.

Then, home to Hope, for whom he prayed every night, and their baby, whom he could not wait to meet.

With these happy thoughts, Heck slipped into contented slumber.

CHAPTER 57

Heck was still examining his new rifle, an 1851 breechloading Sharps that used paper cartridges and fired a .52 caliber, 475 grain bullet, when Mr. Dean returned again, this time accompanied by the would-be buyers and their assistants.

Heck and Sam stood on either side of the scale. They leaned their rifles beside the shovels.

Jim and Two Bits were a short distance off in opposite directions, hidden behind tombstones with their own rifles just in case anyone tried something.

Not that Heck expected any trouble from these handpicked bidders. But one never knew who might show up at a time like this. The only way to really hope for the best was to prepare for the worst.

Seeing *Don* Vasquez among the approaching men, Heck raised a hand.

Vasquez waved in return.

A white-haired man at the edge of the group pointed at Heck and said, "You're the fighter!"

Heck touched his blackened eye and grinned. "What gave it away?"

"I lost a thousand dollars on that fight," the white-haired man declared without any apparent irritation. "You really surprised me."

"He really surprised everyone," declared a portly, bald man with a monocle and a bristling mustache. "I've never seen such a fight. Well done, young man. I, too, lost a good deal of money, but I was certainly entertained."

"You should have bet on Mr. Martin," *Don* Vasquez laughed. "I did."

"Well, that's all good and well for you, Vasquez," said the fourth and final bidder, a tall man whose powerful physique and rugged features clashed with his fancy suit, "but I want to know what you're doing here, Martin. Mr. Dean, if you think you can frighten—"

"I'm the owner," Heck said.

Three of the bidders looked surprised.

The fourth, *Don* Vasquez, threw back his head and laughed.

The tall man looked more irritated than ever. "What's the meaning of all this? Why bring us into a graveyard of all places?"

"To show you the nugget and hold the auction," Heck said.

"Where is it? I don't see it."

"Oh, it's here," Heck said. "In fact, you're standing on it."

The man looked down at the grave beneath his feet, clearly confused.

"I wanted to make sure everyone showed before we dug it up," Heck said.

"Dug it up?"

"Yes, sir," Heck said, grabbing a shovel. "Now, if you'll step aside, we'll get started."

Sam came forward, too, as did the grave diggers he'd hired this morning. The graveyard keeper himself had refused to unearth the casket, though he'd taken the money readily enough and agreed to keep anyone from entering this section of the cemetery.

Heck was glad he had help. His hands were badly swollen and terribly sore. At least he could still move everything. After all, he reckoned he might end up needing to pull a trigger or two before all of this was over.

They started to dig. Since the grave was fresh, it was easy work.

Horrified, the tall man said, "Are you a grave robber?"

"No, sir," Heck said, "I'm cautious."

They dug up the casket, hoisted it free, and broke it open.

The assembly gasped—except *Don* Vasquez, who grinned and said, "You certainly are full of surprises, Mr. Martin."

"To survive in the wilderness," Heck said, "you gotta have a few surprises up your sleeve."

The men stepped forward and stared with awe at the giant nugget sparkling inside the casket.

"How do we know it's real?" the tall man asked.

"What's your name?" Heck said.

The man lifted his chin a little. "I am Percival Dumay."

Heck had suspected as much. Mr. Dean had warned him about Dumay. He was a pain to deal with, a rough-and-tumble gold baron with a dark past who also happened to be the wealthiest man in California.

"Hi, Mr. Dumay," Heck said, holding out his hand. "I'm Heck Martin."

Dumay stared with obvious disgust at Heck's big, dirty, bruised paw then reached out and shook it fleetingly before wiping his fingers on a silk handkerchief quickly handed to him by his assistant.

"Nice to meet you," Heck said. "You know it's real because I give you my word it's real."

Dumay frowned and raised one brow. "I would rather have the word of my assayer, if it's all the same to you, Mr. Martin."

"Go ahead, everyone," Heck said. "Let your assayers take a look. But be careful with it. That nugget is one of a kind."

Each bidder had brought his own assayer. These professionals moved forward, surrounded the casket, and reached inside.

A few seconds later, the assayer accompanying *Don* Vasquez turned and nodded to his employer. "*Oro Sólido.*"

Solid gold.

The other assayers quickly agreed.

Sam and Mr. Dean lugged the scale over, and the bidders were given time to examine and test the scale.

Heck and Sam lifted the nugget out of the casket and sat it on the scale, which registered 103 pounds, 7 ounces.

"There we have it, gentlemen," Mr. Dean said. "You have examined the nugget, determined its purity, and verified its weight. We will begin the bidding at sixteen dollars an ounce. Do we have a bidder?"

All four men raised their hands.

From there, things escalated quickly. These were men of means, men used to having their way, men who conducted business as efficiently as Heck dealt death.

When the price exceeded twenty dollars an ounce, the white-haired man waved them off. "Too rich for my blood."

The bald man dropped out a dollar later.

Vasquez and Dumay, bidding in quarter-dollar increments, cranked the price higher and higher.

"Twenty-five dollars an ounce," *Don* Vasquez said, staring at the pompous Mr. Dumay.

A pleased Heck did the math. At twenty-five dollars an ounce, he was looking at a payday of $41,375. Minus the ten percent he would owe Mr. Dean and the fifteen percent he planned to split evenly between his three traveling companions, that would still leave him with over $31,000.

Dumay yawned dramatically and leapt ahead, ignoring the established increments. "Twenty-six dollars an ounce. Be content with your cattle, Mr. Vasquez, the nugget is mine."

Vasquez shook his head and failed to counter the bid.

"Going once at twenty-six dollars an ounce," Mr. Dean pronounced. "Going twice..."

Seeing *Don* Vasquez's disappointment and Mr. Dumay's satisfied smirk, Heck said, "Fifty dollars an ounce."

"What's the meaning of this?" Dumay snapped. "You can't bid."

"Who says I can't?"

"It's unheard of."

"The bid stands," Mr. Dean said. "Fifty dollars an ounce."

"But that's a ridiculous sum," Dumay said. He hesitated for

two or three seconds and said. "That's eighty-two thousand, seven hundred and fifty dollars!"

"That was some impressive calculation, Mr. Dumay," Heck said. "Do you want to top it or not?"

Dumay flushed, trembling with rage. "I most certainly do not!"

"Going once, going twice," Mr. Dean said. "Sold to Heck Martin for fifty dollars an ounce."

"I'll pay myself later," Heck said. "Now, *Don* Vasquez, I would like to offer you this nugget in a private sale."

The cattleman grinned. "How much?"

"I was thinking twenty-five dollars an ounce—payable in longhorns and the temporary use of your *vaqueros*. I want to run a herd on my land."

Vasquez nodded thoughtfully. "There would be a delay with the cattle. They would come from my ranches in Mexico. From there, I could sell you fine horse as well. The very best, including cattle horses."

"I'm in no hurry to build my herd, and yeah, I'd be interested in horses, too."

Grinning, *Don* Vasquez stuck out his hand. "You have a deal, my friend."

Heck shook, and that was that. As far as he was concerned, the deal was set in stone.

"This is an outrage!" Dumay shouted. "I've never been so insulted in all my life! You haven't heard the last of me, Heck Martin!"

As the irate businessman stormed off, Mr. Dean thanked the other men for participating. "Now, *Don* Vasquez, if we could conclude this transaction quickly, my client has a boat to catch."

CHAPTER 58

"That's it," Bill Getty chuckled darkly, spotting the private vessel Heck Martin had booked for passage to Oregon. "*The Sojourner.* Come on, men. Into the rowboat."

Leo entered first and sat in the prow, holding his trusty shotgun.

Getty's goons followed and took up the oars.

Getty boarded last and took his seat, fondling a pepperbox revolver in his pocket. Not that he planned on shooting the thing. Yes, he had risen to power by cracking skulls and pulling triggers; but now, his goons handled that sort of work.

Though for the celebrated Heck Martin, he might just come out of retirement and take matters into his own hands one last time.

Martin had ruined him.

He'd bet everything on Heller.

And then Martin had knocked Big Jim Heller unconscious. It had been such a devastating knockout that no one, even those who'd unwisely lost their shirts like Getty, could question its validity.

So yes, Martin had ruined him.

But just as Heller had underestimated Martin, Martin had underestimated Getty.

In fact, the fool didn't even know Getty existed.

Soon, he would know him, all right. He would beg Getty for mercy as so many others had in the past.

But you didn't rise to power by showing mercy. You rose to power by banishing all weakness and seizing big opportunities when they came your way.

And this was a big opportunity.

Martin didn't just have Getty's money, after all. He had *everyone's* money. Plus the money he'd bet Heller and whatever he'd gotten from the gate... not to mention the nugget or whatever he'd sold it for.

Terrance had been utterly useless in terms of providing information about the auction.

Oh well. None of that mattered now because Getty and his men were about to board The Sojourner and take everything Heck Martin had, including his miserable life.

There would be time enough for counting later.

The Sojourner moved slowly toward the busy mouth of the harbor, which always kept a lane open for departing vessels.

Getty followed despite the crowd.

Because that was another thing you needed to rise to the top: audacity.

Fools would never dare to make a move like this with so many onlookers.

Getty, on the other hand, knew there was no better time and

place to kill a man than on a crowded street at noon. No one saw it coming, and by the time witnesses recovered from their shock and sorted out what happened, you were long gone, and no one could quite remember, let alone agree on, what you looked like.

So Getty didn't hesitate when the lifeboat bumped into the hull of the larger boat.

"Grapples up," he commanded, and his crew flung their grappling hooks over the rail and found purchase. "Board her, men!"

The goons scaled the ropes and boarded the ship like so many pirates, pistols at the ready.

Leo followed after them, silent as death.

"Keep this boat steady," Getty told the man he'd assigned to do just this task, "or I'll skin you alive."

"Yes, Mr. Getty."

Getty grabbed hold of a rope and climbed nimbly up. He was a short, stocky, thickly muscled man, and he was still strong, even after all these years, still as strong as he'd been back in Five Points, making war with the Dead Rabbits and the Plug Uglies.

He swung over the rail and strode into the cabin, which was full of shouting. He heard the meaty slap of a fist impacting a face.

Feeling a surge of triumph, Getty entered the room.

His joy was short-lived.

"Where is he?" Leo demanded, jamming his shotgun into the captain's belly. "Where's Heck Martin?"

"I got no idea!" the captain said. "He never showed up, so I lifted anchor and set sail. That was the agreement. If he didn't make it in time, I was supposed to head out anyway, no delay. He was very particular on that point. So I headed out without him. And kept the money."

Sudden heat filled Getty's chest and crept up his neck and into his face.

Leo stared at him, slack jawed.

"Search this boat," Getty told his goons. "Tear it apart if you have to. Make sure Martin isn't hiding somewhere."

But he isn't onboard, Getty told himself. *He isn't hiding anywhere. He outsmarted you. He booked this boat for that exact purpose, and you took the bait, and now, he's bought himself a tasty head start.*

"Come on, Leo," he said. "We're going to go kill Heck Martin."

CHAPTER 59

The shadows were growing longer when Heck finally spotted them.

Five hundred yards back, two riders hurtled toward them with reckless abandon.

Greed made fools of men.

Heck reined Red to a stop, raised his spyglasses.

One of the men fit the description Able Dean had provided for Bill Getty.

With Getty was a burly man packing a coach gun. That must be Leo.

"Here they come," Heck announced, pulling his new Sharps from its scabbard.

The thing was pretty neat. Earlier, he'd practiced with it. Reloading the breechloader was new to him—and fast. He figured he could fire it three or four times faster than he could his dearly departed Hawken.

His musings were rudely interrupted when he noticed the

conditions of the would-be robbers' horses. They were both wild-eyed and frothing at the mouth.

Desperate to catch up, Getty had pushed the poor animals to the point of death.

Greed didn't just make fools of men. It made monsters of them.

"How do you want to do this, Heck?" Jim asked.

"No reason to complicate things," Heck said and told them his simple plan. "Let's just get over this next hill."

A short time later, the two riders came charging over the hill... determined to kill Heck and steal his money, no doubt.

"Whoa!" Getty cried, surprised to find the wagon blocking his path, and hauled hard on the reins.

It was too much for his exhausted horse, which collapsed heavily onto its side, pitching Getty from the saddle.

He hit hard, grunting with the impact, and the little pistol he'd been holding discharged with a muffled explosion. Getty cried out in pain.

The fool had shot himself in the guts.

Leo's horse, exhausted beyond repair, jerked in fear, stumbled, and slammed into the wagon.

Leo fell from the saddle but recovered quickly, rolling into a crouch and lifting the stubby scattergun to his shoulder.

Then Two Bits's Hawken roared, and most of Leo's head disappeared.

Heck strode out of the scrub, vaguely disappointed that he hadn't had a chance to fire his new rifle.

Getty lurched onto all fours, turned to his dying steed, and started tugging at the rifle trapped in a scabbard beneath the horse. He grunted, hunching his powerful shoulders, and somehow managed to extract the long-barreled rifle.

He turned, bringing it around, and Heck kicked him in the face.

When Getty came to again, he instantly reached for the rifle only to realize he no longer had it in his possession.

"This is my Hawken," Heck said. "But something tells me you didn't ride all the way out here to return it to me."

Getty, a waterfront tough to the end, didn't make any excuses. Instead, he cursed Heck up one side and down another, throwing in a few death threats for good measure.

"Able Dean told me about all the people you've killed," Heck said. "Or at least the ones in San Francisco. He thinks you killed a bunch more back in New York, and I'd have to guess he's right, but I'm a merciful man by nature. I might have dismissed those facts, might have forgotten all the trouble you caused me in town, might even have forgiven you for riding out to kill me and my friends and take our money, but you know what I can't forgive? I can't forgive a man who rides his horse to death. Just what sort of monster are you?"

Then, suddenly, Getty showed him, stuffing a boxy hand into a pocket and jerking it back out with a derringer.

Getty was quick. Heck had to give him that. The man hadn't hesitated at all. When he'd decided to go for it, he'd gone for it. The pistol was lifting toward its target when Heck's rifle and three others boomed, ridding the waterfront and the world at large of a notorious villain.

CHAPTER 60

Looking down into the crib at the sleeping baby, Heck felt like his heart might burst from love. He'd never been so happy in his whole life.

My son, he thought, staring down at the dark-haired infant and feeling a visceral connection of staggering power. *I would do anything for you.*

Beside him, Hope dabbed at her eyes and smiled so brightly it was a wonder it didn't wake the baby.

She tugged at Heck's sleeve and whispered, "Come on, Daddy. Let's go talk."

"Just a second," Heck said and leaned in to kiss the eight-week-old on the forehead.

His son stirred, smacked his tiny lips, and slid back into deep slumber.

Heck and Hope retreated to the little porch that someone had built them in Heck's absence. It was rough but nice.

Ten minutes earlier, when Heck had arrived home after a

nearly three-month absence, he had been stunned by Hope City. Not just by the new buildings—and there were many—but also by the great number of people here, most of whom, he understood from his brief conversation with Doc, wanted to stay.

Hope City was becoming an honest to goodness town, which raised all sorts of possibilities and potential problems— but he pushed these from his mind now, focusing solely on his family.

Everyone and everything else could just wait.

"I am stunned," Heck confessed. "It doesn't even seem possible to love someone so much the first time you saw them."

"I felt the same way, Heck, from the moment he was born, and I love him more each day. Do you want to know his name?"

"Of course, I want to know his name," Heck said, laughing and shaking his head. "I was so excited to see you two, I forgot to even ask."

"Your son's name is Hector Martin III. Since you're Heck, we call him Tor for short."

"Tor?"

"That's right. If you don't like it, we—"

"I love it, Hope. Tor Martin. Sounds like he's gonna be a great man."

"We'll do our best to raise him right, anyway."

"Yes, we will," he said and kissed her. "Hope, I am so sorry I wasn't here for the birth. I prayed for you both every day and—"

"Heck Martin," she said, "don't you dare apologize to me. You did what you had to do, and I did what I had to do."

"How did it go for you? Were you all right?"

"I won't lie. I was scared." She squeezed his hand. "For a while, I had a pretty hard time—childbirth is *painful*—but there were no complications, praise God, and in the end, everything was all right."

"Yes, praise God," Heck said. "But I sure am sorry I left you alone."

"I wasn't alone. Veronica was a wonderful midwife, and Mother stayed with me every step of the way. From what I understand, Doc paced in front of the cabin the whole time in case there was a problem." She lifted a hand and rubbed it across Heck's cheek, which he had just shaved again that morning. "I can't believe you shaved your beard."

"Well, I did. Don't you like me clean-shaven?"

"I love it, Heck. I absolutely love it. I just can't get over how handsome you look."

"You keep talking like that, my beautiful wife, and I'm gonna take you inside and—"

"Heck!" she laughed, slapping his arm. "That sort of talk is not suited for the front porch."

He smiled at her. "Well, you just consider yourself warned, little lady."

"You don't scare me, Heck Martin. If anyone should be warned, it's you. I've been missing you something awful this whole time. I hope you still have your strength after the long trip."

"Oh, I've got plenty of strength. I'll show you tonight."

"I can't wait. In the meantime, what's the news? Tell me everything that happened."

"Well, this happened," Heck said, pulling the deed from his haversack.

"What's this?"

"It's the deed for this valley."

"Already?"

"That's right. Just like Jim Bridger said, Able Dean is a good man."

Hope's eyes flicked across the lines. "Your name, mine, Seeker's—I'm so glad you included him, Heck."

"Of course."

Then her mouth dropped open. "Is this a mistake?"

He grinned. "Is what a mistake?"

"Fifteen thousand, three hundred and sixty acres?"

"That's no mistake. That's how much ground we own, Hope. All in, it's twenty-four square miles. Everything we'd wanted plus an extra mile to the north and two extra miles to the south, which secures the grassy valleys. East to west, we're also wider. Two miles each way. So six miles tall and four miles wide, though we have to allow an easement for the Oregon Trail."

For a second, Hope just blinked at him. "I'm stunned, Heck. I mean, this is wonderful news... but how?"

"That, my love, is a long story," he said.

"Tell me."

"I will. And I want to know everything that happened here, especially with you and Tor—but first..."

He drew her close and wrapped his arms around her and kissed her forehead and laid his head against hers. They had a lot of work in front of them and more than a little trouble headed their way, he knew, but now was not the time to consider those things.

"First, I just want to be with you," he said. "I just want to sit and hold you and praise Jesus for bringing me home to my beautiful wife and our healthy baby boy."

#

THANK YOU FOR READING *HECK'S GOLD*.

Heck and Hope's adventures continue in *Heck's Gamble*.

If you enjoyed this story, please be a friend and leave a review. When you leave even a short review, you just bought my family dinner, because Amazon will show the book to more people. I sure would appreciate your help.

If you enjoyed the book but don't have time to review, please consider leaving a 5-star rating. It's quick and simple and helps me get this new series off the ground.

I love Westerns and hope to bring you 8 or 10 a year. To hear about new releases, special sales, and giveaways, join my reader list.

Once more, thanks for reading. I hope our paths cross again.

Until then, don't approach a bull from the front, a horse from the rear, or a fool from any direction.

John

ABOUT THE AUTHOR

I was born six months before man landed on the moon and lucky enough to grow up in the country, where my family lived largely off the land.

When I wasn't fishing, exploring the woods, or weeding the garden, I devoured comic books like *Two-Gun Kid* and *The Rawhide Kid* before moving on to the exciting adventure stories of Jack London and Louis L'Amour.

Our black-and-white TV only got three channels, though you could lose one and pick up another if you went outside and messed with the antenna. On its grainy screen, we watched *Gunsmoke*, *Bonanza*, and movies starring John Wayne and Clint Eastwood.

Now a husband and father, I love traveling the West and reading history and fiction alike. My favorite authors are Louis L'Amour, Elmore Leonard, C.J. Petit, and R.O. Lane.

As a writer, I hope to entertain you with fun stories of the old West. My good guys are good, my bad guys are bad, and you'll always find a touch of romance to sweeten the grit.

If you'd like to keep in touch, join my newsletter HERE.